GETTING THE PICTURE

GETTING
THE
PICTURE

A NOVEL

Sarah Salway

Ballantine Books Trade Paperbacks
New York

A Ballantine Books Trade Paperback Original

Copyright © 2010 by Sarah Salway

Published in the United States by Ballantine Books, an imprint of The Random House Publishing Group, a division of Random House, Inc., New York.

BALLANTINE and colophon are registered trademarks of Random House, Inc.

ISBN 978-0-345-48101-6

Printed in the United States of America

www.ballantinebooks.com

2 4 6 8 9 7 5 3 1

Book design by Karin Batten

To Francis

Old ladies must never be crossed: in their hands
lie the reputations of the young ones.

—PIERRE AMBROISE FRANÇOIS CHODERLOS DE LACLOS,
Les Liaisons dangereuses

GETTING THE PICTURE

Once Upon a Time

The studio was just a room over a newsagent's shop.

When her friend had told her about a photographer she'd met at a nightclub and what he'd asked her to do, Maureen begged to be allowed to come too. She'd pictured something different—lots of mirrors with those Hollywood lightbulbs around them; walls of purple or red suede; jazz music playing in the background; strange beautiful men and women smoking long cigarettes as they lounged on uncomfortable furniture. Maybe even a lion cub like the one in the photograph of an American film star she'd seen in a magazine once.

No lions here. The only other person in the room was the photographer and he was far more interested in fiddling around with the equipment than talking to them. First of all, he placed these huge white umbrellas on the bare floorboards to surround what she presumed was the set, a chair placed on white pieces of paper laid out on the floor. There were several colored blankets, which the photographer draped up against the white plastered walls. One corner was curtained off.

"You can undress in there," he told Pat. "There's a gown hanging up for you to slip into."

Maureen wanted to follow, but there wasn't enough room behind the curtains for two so she stayed outside. She walked over to the photographs pinned up on the wall until she registered they were all of naked women and looked away quickly. The photographer had his back to her; he was putting on a record now, blowing at it first to remove some imaginary dust. Her husband did that. But then there was a screech as the photographer cleaned the needle with his fingers. Her husband definitely didn't do that. The grainy voice of Elvis Presley sang out. Maureen knew she was supposed to love him, all her friends did, but there was something animal about him that frightened her.

At least the photographer was small. Small and young, and a bit shabby in his blue sweater and jeans. If the worse came to the worst, she and Pat would be able to overpower him between them. She went back to the curtain and tugged on it, hissing, to get her friend's attention.

"Are you sure you want to go through with this?" Maureen asked.

Elvis sang from the other corner about fevers.

"You bet. It'll be a laugh," Pat called out. Her voice was muffled, as if her dress was covering her mouth. Which it would be if she really was getting undressed. "Are you sure you don't want to have a go?"

Maureen grimaced. "Not me. I can just imagine what my old man would say. He'd be bound to find out, although—"

At the thought of George buying the sort of magazine these

photographs would appear in, Maureen burst into giggles. The port and lemon must be kicking in.

"We are naughty being here," she said.

When no response came, she went back to stare at the wall of photographs. The women in them looked so happy, as if they lived in a different land from the one she knew. A happy-women land where no shopping needed to be done, no children needed looking after, no men to moan at or to chase, no chores to never quite catch up on. One woman wore a beret, long dangly diamond earrings and a necklace, thick black stockings, high heels, but nothing else. The trumpet she was playing covered nearly everything. Another was on a swing, her head back, neck arched toward a window that seemed familiar. Maureen looked around the studio curiously, and yes, there was the swing hanging from the corner beam. She hadn't been in a kiddies' playground for years. Her daughter, Nell, was still a bit young for that, but she used to love going on the swing herself. George was more of a slide man, a brisk up and down, but Maureen had always liked the gentle to and fro, the way you could watch the clouds drift over you, never sure if it were you or them moving.

She tried to sway with the music. At home, they normally listened to singers her husband preferred, ones like Dean Martin and Frank Sinatra. Pat said it was because George was frightened you could get arrested from listening to the new bands like the Beatles. Although Maureen laughed at the way Pat imitated George—"where will it end?"—it wasn't fair, really. Pat was free so she could do what she wanted, even go to the America she was always rattling on about. George had her and the baby to look after.

"So, Blondie, you don't fancy being a model, then?"

She twirled around to find the photographer behind her, a camera slung around his neck. His name was Martin, although Pat said they should call him Mart. That felt a bit informal to

Maureen. Overfriendly. He had a nice smile and an easy manner, but there was something about the way he was looking at her now that made her want to take a step back.

"I'm a mother." She made a strange grimace, trying to make a joke of it to show she was comfortable being there. "Who'd want to see me naked?"

She surprised herself by not mentioning what her husband might say this time. But what shocked her more was her disappointment when Martin didn't disagree with her. He just nodded, turned toward the curtain and started calling, "Trisha, Trisha, come out, my lovely girl, my Camberwell beauty, my pearly queen," gently, almost caressingly, so that when Pat did come out, a red silk gown wrapped tightly around her, laughing, pink-cheeked, Maureen saw her friend had already turned into one of the happy-women-land women of the photographs. Pat sat down on the chair with the aplomb of someone who did this sort of thing regularly. The photographer went over and draped a red blanket over the chair, standing back and then adjusting it some more. He handed Pat a book.

"Do you want to slip the gown halfway off your shoulders, and pretend to be reading?" he asked, but Pat looked straight across at her. She didn't seem embarrassed though, as Maureen would have been in her situation.

"My friend, Mo, doesn't approve," Pat said, still staring at Maureen, the gown slipping off one shoulder. She exaggerated the "Mo" because it was the name Maureen had said she'd use if she ever plucked up the courage to have her photograph taken. Pat said she'd be Trisha, because it was the one shortening of her name her mother had always hated. "It took several drinks just to get her here," Pat continued, "and now she's looking at me as if she's not stopped sucking the lemon."

"Pat! That's not fair."

"Not everyone can have a body like yours." Martin ignored

Maureen and leaned in toward Pat. "You're peachy, Trisha. Like Venus. That's what I want to catch, that look of yours, just as if you're going to put down the book, stand up, hold out your hand and take me to your bedroom. Go on. Show me what it would be like to be the luckiest man alive."

Maureen stomped over to the alcove and drew the curtain across sharply. After she'd brushed Pat's clothes off the chair, she sat down to wait. The studio could do with a good sweep and clean. And she'd bet the woman in the photograph didn't really know how to play the trumpet. She put her foot out and placed it on Pat's minidress, smiling when she saw the dusty footprint it left. It was too short for Pat anyway, with her porky legs. From the other side of the curtain, she could hear the chatter, the occasional burst of laughter, the scraping of the chair as it was moved around and, as if underlining it all, the *click-click-click* of the lens. Maureen lifted her legs off the ground and held them in front of her, imagining she was on the swing. She arched her back, took out her clips and felt the weight of her long hair as she let her head drop. Then she sat up again and ran her open palms down her body, feeling where her hipbones still jutted and her breasts were still firm, even after having a child. But she couldn't stop thinking that no matter how many times George might say he appreciated her, luck wouldn't play any part in his thoughts. She was his wife, the bed thing just part of the marriage contract.

She heard Pat giggle again. An annoying high-pitched titter that she'd never noticed before but she knew would grate on her nerves now. She should never have come. Pat hadn't even particularly wanted her to. She was just full of Mart, Mart, Mart. Martin printed his own magazines, apparently. Sold them to newsagents like the one downstairs who kept them under the counter. There was a huge market. Photographs of women for men to dream about, but Pat said everything was done nicely. And apparently, he was going to make films. He had contacts. He'd told Pat she could be a film star if the photographs turned out well. She'd go to her precious America even. Mart, Mart, Mart.

Maureen peered into the mirror. Under her thick bangs, she could make out a white tense face and shoulders rising up to meet her ears. Maybe it wasn't a reflection to inspire dreams, but she was still young, wasn't she? What with looking after George and Nell, she forgot that sometimes. She thought about the photographer's eyes. They'd been gray, that unusual color that made you think of the British seaside. She'd noticed them when he stared right into her eyes while they were talking. He hadn't looked down at her chest or over her shoulder as men normally did.

She heard Pat laughing again, and Martin was saying something about it being a good shoot, she was a good model, the best model, a sweetheart of a girl.

Maureen drew back the curtains and stepped out into the studio. Pat had the gown wrapped tightly around her, and the photographer was stooped over the camera, his back toward them.

"You can take my picture now if you want," Maureen said roughly. "Not naked though. And if Pat hasn't used up all the film in the camera, of course."

Martin put his head to one side and stared at her. Pat did her giggle again as she walked past to the changing cubicle. But Maureen stood still, unsmiling, chin raised, hands fisted by her thighs. She waited until she heard the swish of the curtain behind Pat.

"Just one, mind," Maureen said. "And you have to take it as I am. I'm not taking my clothes off."

He lifted the camera, put it to his eye and clicked. Then he reached across and with the lightest touch of his fingertips, he ran them across her cheekbone, backward and forward. A butterfly kiss.

"Mo, is it?" he asked, and she nodded. For some reason, she wanted to cry. "You're a beautiful woman, Mo," he said.

"That's what you say to all the girls, Martin," Pat called out from behind the curtain. "But we love you for it." Maureen winced as she waited for the giggle.

Martin shook his head, and put one finger against Maureen's lips so she couldn't say anything. She raised her hand to his, as if to keep it there. She was right. His eyes were gray like the sea out of season, with flecks of light brown like sand. A shifting tide.

By the time Pat came out of the changing room, Maureen was standing at the door, ready to go. She clattered down the stairs, and waited for Pat outside in the street.

"You're awful quiet," Pat said as they walked to the bus stop together. "Cat got your tongue? At least old George has got nothing to worry about. You're a good girl. Not like me, eh?" She let out a hoot of laughter.

Maureen shook her head. Her hands were thrust deep in her raincoat pockets, the fingers of the right one were playing with a ball of paper, as if they could make out the telephone number Martin had scribbled out for her just before she'd left.

The worst thing about swings, she remembered, was how, when you were going really high, the ground below seemed to turn to water so it became frightening to step back onto firm ground. You wanted to stay swinging forever, suspended in midair.

1. LETTER FROM DR. MICHAEL CROFT TO BRENDA LEWIS, HOUSE MANAGER, PILGRIM HOUSE

Dear Mrs. Lewis,

Please find enclosed the medical details for my patient, Martin Morris, who moved successfully into Pilgrim House with you on Monday.

Although there have been situations in the past that have been of concern, he has no current medical problems. You will notice, however, that he has a tendency to introspection. I am hopeful that the varied social program at Pilgrim House will encourage him to form social links and that this will have a beneficial effect on his health. He is, as you pointed out in your assessment, young to be in an establishment like yours, but unfortunately a lifetime of personal neglect has taken its toll. He has never married, and has no immediate family. His landlord, Mahad Jefferies, has always kept an eye on him, but he will shortly be retiring to Birmingham to live with his daughter's family.

I should say Mr. Morris has been very concerned about whether, should he change his mind, he could leave Pilgrim House. I have assured him that it is a home he will be living in, not a prison. However, in any discussion with him about this it is important to remember that Mr. Jefferies has sold the shop and therefore Martin no longer has a room to move back to.

Yours sincerely,
Michael Croft

2. LETTER FROM MARTIN MORRIS TO MO GRIFFITHS

Dear Mo,

Do you remember that first time we met? It was in the old studio on Brunson Road. The look on your face was so fierce that I wanted to take you in my arms right then and there and tell you everything was going to be all right with the world. There was no need to fight anymore.

We've been through it all over the years, haven't we, angel? Had more than our fair share of heartbreak. And here I am writing to you at the start of a new adventure. You'll laugh because it's an old people's home. Me—finally living with other people. Old ones at that. I never thought I'd see the day. Well, I hoped I wouldn't.

It's just that I was listening to this music on the radio. A proper concert with black tie and everything. Of course, you couldn't see what they were wearing but the class shone through. You would have loved it. And it was coming from one of the new flats they've built opposite. They are a bunch of yuppies there, but this music was beautiful. I pulled my chair over to the open window to listen. It was like being a bird, floating up above everything and everyone. And then, daft old fool that I am, I started to cry, thinking how you and I had never danced. And probably you never danced without me either, stuck with that dry stick of a husband of yours. How much did we miss, love, by not being together?

So the next morning I went to my doctor and said, put me away. He's young enough to have been our grandchild, although I don't think any child of ours would be a doctor. More a painter, or a poet. Anyway, although he was relieved because he's been on about my so-called options for a bit, he was surprised when I told him I wanted to come to Pilgrim House, and that I wouldn't go anywhere else. Although he said not to get my hopes up, he rang then and there, and it so happened there was a place just come open. I had a feeling in my veins that it would be OK because there's a reason why I need to come here. One I don't think you'll like. You see, George is here. Your husband, George.

I just need to understand what he had that I didn't. Of course I know you had to look after the girls, Nell, and then later Angie, but it wasn't the same as being with me, was it? And I had no one. All those years with no one to talk to.

Anyway, I'll tell you more later. I wanted you to know where I was, Mo. In case you were wondering. And no need to worry about how well I'm being looked after. We live like lords here. Every minute of the day there's someone coming around to boss me about. Have you taken your pill? Have you done a BM today (excuse my language, angel, that's what we call bowel movements here and they seem awfully fond of talking about them). Or else they remind us it's supper in fifteen minutes, or music classes, or special talks. The other folks here say we get the children from the local schools visiting us so often it's a wonder there's any time left over for them to learn how to read and write.

The children are about the only thing I'm looking forward to, but they've only come once since I've been here. "He's a photographer," the matron told them. I liked that, it must have been what the doctor told her. Better than a shop assistant, anyway. So when they asked me to take their pictures, I pretended. I've still got my cameras but I don't put film in them anymore, Mo. I stopped all that a long time ago. But it feels good to lift the camera up sometimes, to feel its weight against my cheek and to be able to catch a certain glint in the eye. Trouble is I see you too often in the viewfinder. That look on your face I can't get rid of.

I'll write later, but everything will be all right, Mo darling. Haven't I always promised you that when you are with me, you didn't have to worry about anything anymore? That's my job.

M

3. LETTER FROM GEORGE GRIFFITHS TO BRENDA LEWIS

Dear Mrs. Lewis,

Once again the soap is missing from the hand basin in my room. I have told you on numerous occasions that another resident, Florence Oliver, is stealing it. This is an intolerable situation and I would be grateful if you could take action with immediate effect.

Yours sincerely,
George Griffiths

4. LETTER FROM FLORENCE OLIVER TO LIZZIE CORN

Dear Lizzie,

That was kind of you to send me the spare photographs of young Brian's birthday party. I thought he had a real look of your Frank about him, especially when he was holding that dagger to the other little boy's face. I'm glad you told me it was plastic because it looks dangerously close to the eyes. And I wonder how they could fit so many children on the trampoline! No wonder Laurie was frightened it might collapse. Good of her to make the birthday tea so healthy, although I don't see what's so wrong with a bit of cake. Still, if you think Brian really didn't mind the carrots. I just think young mums these days make so much work for themselves. But hark at me. As you have so often told me, I don't understand what it's like to be a mother.

Meanwhile, here in the land of the living dead, a new man has arrived, not that you'd know. Not like George Griffiths. His room is plum in the middle of everything, and you can hear *him* stomping around even when you don't want to, but it's like this new man floats. He's always suddenly appearing in corners and giving us a shock. Beth Crosbie says he gives her the heebie-jeebies. Mind, you remember me telling you about her. She's the one who is still married but her husband lives out. In a flat. Does for himself and everything, although of course she's been too ill to help for a long time. He was practically looking after her himself for years. Strange thing for a man to do, although he still fusses all the time about her. He's the one who made them take up her carpet and put a pink one in. Everything gives her the h-j's. It's not just me who says she's self-indulgent. Catherine Francis, the one who gets the bus into town every Friday to have tea at Hoopers, she says Beth should just pull herself together.

But that's the problem of having a man around to care for you. You give in. We know all about that, don't we, pet? Just think how many adventures we've had by ourselves since our husbands, God bless them, passed on. Take that time at the bingo in Portsmouth when that woman accused you of cheating after you called the Full House, and we had to run along the pier to get away from her. How we laughed. Well, we did when we were safely back in the B&B enjoying our Ovaltine. I just think about us being able to run anywhere now and I'm amazed. Seems like a different life.

Still, mustn't get gloomy. It must be time for us to start planning my next trip to you soon. Do let me know when Laurie thinks it convenient to spare you.

We had a very interesting speaker here the other night. The young man's mother, Joan, runs the corner shop, and when Brenda was getting some bits and bobs in there, Joan was boasting how he'd just won some big essay-writing competition at his university. So he came in to talk to us about Virginia Woolf. It gave us all such a lovely nap and then when we woke up, Brenda made us a nice cup of tea.

Anyway, this comes, as always, with many best wishes to you and your family. I hope your cold is better. A nasty thing, a cold is.

You don't go out without drying your hair, do you? That often brings on a cold and yours do seem to linger.

Yours aye,
Florence

P.S. Naughty of Brian though to steal your stockings for his bandit costume. Did Laurie really not tell him off?

5. NOTE FROM FLORENCE OLIVER TO GEORGE GRIFFITHS

I have not touched your precious soap. Nor would I want to. If you tell Matron any more lies about me, I will call the police.

6. NOTE FROM GEORGE GRIFFITHS TO NELL BAKER (LEFT ON RECEPTION DESK AT PILGRIM HOUSE)

Dear Nell,

It is now 8:10 a.m. and I have been waiting for you at reception for the last ten minutes. When you finally arrive, you may find me in my room. You know the value I put on punctuality so I have to say I'm disappointed.

Your father

7. LETTER FROM MARTIN MORRIS TO MO GRIFFITHS

Dear Mo,

Well, here I am, angel, a bit more settled in. I have the smallest room in the house, but it suits me fine because I'm right up at the top, out of the way. If I stand in the middle of the room, I can touch two of the walls with both hands. And when I'm in my narrow monk's bed, tucked away under the eaves, it's possible to put my hand up and feel the ceiling. It's a nook, a nest, a haven. It reminds me of my studio.

I have a bed, a wardrobe, a chair, a little shelf and a washbasin. That's all. That's all I want. Nothing on the walls, nothing specially placed to "cheer the place up." I've tucked my boxes of photographs away under my bed along with the box containing these letters. All safe. And no one comes into my room. I couldn't bear to feel that someone might spy on me. It's like the studio. Once I stopped the photography, only Mahad was allowed up the stairs and never through the door.

I did a thorough search the first night before I went to sleep. I knew there'd be a sign of the room's last occupant left somewhere. It took time because I wasn't sure what I was looking for, but then, just as I was about to give up, I found it. Tucked away at the back of one of the shelves in the little pine wardrobe, there was a toffee wrapper. All twisted and tied up in a knot. I picked it up by the very edge and put it in the bin. "Good-bye, Tom Pardoe," I said as I dropped it. He was a quiet man, apparently. Only here a couple of months before they moved him to the hospice, but it still felt like some kind of ceremony was needed to get rid of his presence.

If this is going to be my last home, I want it uncluttered and clear. I want to be able to concentrate on what's always mattered the most in my life. You and me.

I have a window, though. I can see the little strips of lawns from left to right, all with red-bricked walls separating them. I haven't seen the neighbors on the right, and from the look of their lawn, they don't use it much, but there are two young brothers on the left-hand side. I hide behind my curtains because they climb up on the wall when they think no one's watching and throw stones at our rosebushes. What is it with small boys and the need to hit things?

And the other day I saw one of them holding something up to his eyes that they kept passing from one to another. I couldn't see what it was at first, but then I realized they'd made some binoculars out of toilet rolls. They were watching Brenda Lewis hang out the washing. She shooed them away when she spotted them, but as soon as she'd gone, they popped up again. They were laughing and trying to push each other off the wall, and then they threw something at Brenda's washing. They kept dipping down and throwing again several times before I realized it was handfuls of mud they were chucking. I think they were trying to knock the washing off the line. After a bit, they went quiet and just sat straddling the wall, watching how the underwear swayed in the wind through those cardboard binoculars of theirs.

I wonder what they thought was interesting enough to spy on. Perhaps they were thinking what a strange species we are to wear such giant underpants.

They call us the Pilgrims around here, which feels apt. We're all in some kind of limbo station on our journey toward death. Most like me are going about it as quietly as we can, and yet this still makes us something of interest. To those boys, it seems we are of great interest.

I haven't spoken to George yet. You might wonder how that could be when we're in the same house, but we both keep to ourselves. I've seen one of your daughters though. Nell. And Robyn, the granddaughter. She's a good-looking girl. A Goth, if you know what that is. I used to rather like them coming into the newsagents, like little butterflies of doom. It seems that Angie is in France. I'm biding my time. It's not as if I don't have any to spare.

M

8. NOTE FROM GEORGE GRIFFITHS TO BRENDA LEWIS

Dear Mrs. Lewis,

You may not be aware that yesterday afternoon when you were absent, Susan Reed's daughter visited, along with the family dog.

Not only did the dog bark several times, but I watched it relieve itself on the front lawn.

I have looked up the regulations for Pilgrim House and it specifically says No Pets. I would be grateful if you could bring this to the attention of all residents.

Yours sincerely,
George Griffiths

9. EMAIL FROM NELL BAKER TO ANGIE GRIFFITHS

Hey Angie,

I am at my wit's end with Dad and you've got to help me. Paris is not that far away and he's your father too. You can't keep this noninvolvement thing going forever. He's got worse, if possible. He even talks about himself in the third person. He said to me yesterday: *George Griffiths has never put up with shoddy behavior from anyone, and he's not about to begin now.* I nearly said, *Well, Nell Baker doesn't either,* but old habits and all that. All he wants to talk about is you and your great job. You have to tell him the truth, or I will. I'm tired of biting my lip when he's so rude about Robyn. It's not easy being a single parent, or any kind of parent at all. But you wouldn't know about that, would you?

I will wait to hear when you can come over but make it soon. Please. You have responsibilities here, Angie. Whether you like it or not.

Nell

10. NOTE FROM CLAUDE BICHOURIE TO
ANGELA GRIFFITHS (LEFT ON HOTEL BEDSIDE TABLE)

Chérie,

You looked so beautiful this morning I didn't have the heart to wake you. Here is a little gift for you to buy something nice. I will call you when I can get away, but until then, one hundred kisses everywhere. The hotel bill is paid, of course. I would like to think of you enjoying champagne in bed for breakfast. Indulge me.

Claude

11. LETTER FROM MARTIN MORRIS TO MO GRIFFITHS

Darling Mo,

How did you put up with him for all those years?

I still haven't passed much more than a sentence with George, but I'm already sick of his moaning and bossing and groaning and I don't know what-ing. For years after you'd gone, I'd sit alone upstairs in the studio and think of you at home. I always thought of you happy, angel, even though it would hurt. I imagined you sitting on his knee, him all tired from business-work and you sweet and warm. The two little girls running around, and everyone so cozy. It would make me sick. Physically sick. Not surprising that a drink or two was the only thing that would see me through. I'm not condoning what I did, especially when the drinks crept up. But I looked for comfort where I could find it. And I managed to stop, didn't I? Eventually, I quit drinking, thanks to Mahad, and I made some kind of life for myself.

But the truth is, now I know him, I can't see you with this man. I don't like to upset you but I don't think he is good to his daughter, your daughter, either. The other day she came to call. Early in the morning it was, she must have been up at the crack of dawn to be here, but apparently she was five minutes late. Five minutes, and he'd already left the reception in a sulk. Mrs. Oliver, she's one of the residents here, she was in the sitting room with me and she said he's often like that. Apparently, everything has to be perfect or he creates a scene. And then later, we watched the two of them, George and Nell, from the window. They were walking around the yard as if a black cloud were hanging over them. As if it were an effort for a father to spend time with his daughter.

She looked so tired. It was hard to see you in her. But when I tried, I found a trace of your smile. It would be good to bring it out again, for your sake, Mo.

You see I think of you daily. I think of you hourly. I have never got out of the habit and I have never wanted to. And now I will be able to tell you all about your family. How they are getting on. Even Angie in Paris. I hear he's proud of her, at least. The other residents say she's all he talks about. So I will find out when she's coming to visit and don't fret. I will make things better for you here, angel. I will look after your girls for you.

M

12. LETTER FROM FLORENCE OLIVER TO LIZZIE CORN

Dear Lizzie,

I didn't mean to imply anything rude about Laurie's cooking. It's just that when we were five, we might not have thought bits of cut-up carrots and cucumber was an exciting birthday tea. But I take your point about allergies. And also how the wrong food can get children excited. There is so much to think about nowadays that we didn't have to bother with. Don't let's be cross with each other. You know I don't like it.

We could have used your Laurie's food yesterday when Susan Reed's family came to visit. Although it's nice to have some life about the place, the two grandsons are a bit wild. They made straight for Martin, the new man. They asked him if it was true he used to have photographs in magazines. He went a bit quiet, but then he said that was right. I had no idea. What if he was famous, or something, like the one who married Princess Margaret when she had that teeny waist? And now I come to look at him again, he does have a distinguished air about him.

He wouldn't show them the photographs he'd taken, although he went off to his room and came back with his camera. He spent a long time with them showing how it all worked. He even let them take some pictures themselves, although he told me secretly that there was no film in it. It wasn't one of those modern cameras like your Laurie's. I can't imagine you on a computer, Lizzie, but you are so with-it nowadays.

They pretended to take a photograph of me. I put my hand up to my hair and said, "Do I look beautiful?"

"No," the young one replied, all serious and polite. "You are too creased."

"Say good-bye now," Susan Reed's daughter told them then. "Time to go to the park." I think she thought I'd be upset but I wasn't, because you'll never guess what happened afterward when it was only me, Martin, and George Griffiths left in the sitting room. George was going on about noise and how they'd spoiled his *Daily Telegraph* when they sat on it by accident, but Martin ignored him and leaned across to me. "I think you look beautiful," he said.

I went all peculiar. Even George Griffiths shut up for a moment. Don't you worry, I'm not going to get silly again like I did with that man who came around selling roses at the Blackpool B&B, but I can't remember the last time anyone said I looked beautiful. Or even looked at me.

Anyway, listen to me. There's no fool like an old fool. When I come to you, let's plan our next trip away. I was wondering about

Swanage. Helen Elliott said she once went there with her husband. They stayed in a hotel facing the beach, and when they came back from a walk, the chambermaid was asleep in their bed. Apart from that, Helen said it was very restorative and you get chocolates put on your pillow every night. It would be worth going just for that. There are some good mini breaks advertised in our local paper so I will look out for some bargains. It'll do me good to get away from here for a bit.

Yours aye,
Florence

P.S. What a pity young Brian has caught your cold. I've always found a slurp of whiskey in tomato soup is a great cure. I suppose Laurie will think Brian is too young for whiskey, although it would make him sleep, which might take a weight off her shoulders. And it's full of healthy things. I remember my Graham telling the Colonel's wife that once when she'd asked if he hadn't had enough. He was furious with her, but of course he couldn't show it. Not until we got home, anyway. Still nothing unnatural about nature's goodness, so Laurie might not mind that. Wishing you all well.

13. ANSWER PHONE MESSAGE FROM
GEORGE GRIFFITHS TO ANGIE GRIFFITHS

Dear Angela,

This is your father, George Griffiths, here, talking to your answer phone from England. It's four thirty-five on Tuesday afternoon, Angie. I was thinking it might be more convenient for you to give me your work number. I have called your home several times already and I cannot always get to the phone to receive your calls here. Sadly, I do not trust anyone to pass on the messages you have no doubt left.

I am ringing about Nell. She misses you. I am concerned about her and also about young Robyn. She seems to be running wild to me, and for all her virtues, we can hardly say Nell is a disciplinarian. I try to help but I think Robyn needs a woman's sense. It's at times like this we miss your mother.

So, Angie, it's four thirty-eight now and I would be grateful to hear from you. I know you are busy, of course, but this is your father. George Griffiths. Can you call him back? Call your father, I mean. Me. Good-bye.

14. EMAIL FROM NELL BAKER TO ANGIE GRIFFITHS

I suppose I should thank you for the flowers, Angie, but honestly, how bloody tactless of you to send them to work. Now everyone thinks I've got some secret admirer. Even the work experience girl said "how nice" as if it was all a bit of a joke, and the security guard keeps winking at me. What on earth has Dad been telling you? Why don't you just pick up the phone and speak to him like a normal daughter instead of sending him all those postcards? Well, I guess I know the answer to that one. Dad's not exactly a normal father, is he? But Angie, whatever happened between you and Mum must be over by now. I can't always pick up your pieces.

Your card that came with the flowers was the limit. I do not need to remember to breathe, thank you very much. Do you never think? What I need is some help with Dad, not expensive flowers or stupid advice. When can I tell him you are coming?

15. LETTER FROM GEORGE GRIFFITHS TO BRENDA LEWIS

Dear Mrs. Lewis,

Further to the unpleasant incident in the sitting room last night, I have drafted a timetable for watching television that I feel might create a more appropriate viewing pattern for us all.

Although I appreciate that the fairer sex outweighs my own at

Pilgrim House, I still do not see why we should be subjected to numerous repeats of so-called celebrities pretending to dance. The fact that the only other male resident does not apparently mind this rubbish does not, I believe, come into the equation.

You will see I have divided the grid by the number of viewing hours in a day, and the number of residents. I have checked the newspaper and worked out the average length of programs, and although it may be that we sometimes have to miss the start or end of certain shows, this seems to be a small price to pay for fairness.

Yours sincerely,
George Griffiths

16. LETTER FROM FLORENCE OLIVER TO LIZZIE CORN

Dear Lizzie,

Sit yourself down. I have news. Bit of excitement all around, I can tell you.

Lady F (the one who gets the bus every Friday) asked Susan Reed how she knew about Martin's photographs being in the magazines. Well, Susan's sister, remember her, the one with the teeth and even more grandchildren than Susan, well, her sister has a home help and she told her, the home help told Susan's sister, that she'd been packing up for someone who was coming here. Of course, Susan asked, "What's he like?" because she knew it must have been Martin. Well, you'll never guess but he's a pornographer. Yes, that's right. We knew he was a photographer but not what sort. Apparently he's got two whole boxes of photographs of nude women that he's lugged here with him.

Fancy someone like that saying I was beautiful. I know I should mind, but I don't. Is that very bad of me?

Helen Elliott says we should complain, but she's only saying that because she thinks it's what Lady F wants to hear, and so far, Lady F is giving him the benefit of the doubt. But the funny thing is that the home help said they weren't bad photographs. Not like the nasty muck they have today. She said the women were very tastefully arranged, and besides, most were in black-and-white, which we all agreed makes things better.

And here is something else interesting. He also has a box of envelopes which are addressed and sealed but not sent. It makes you think, doesn't it? Helen says that men never write letters so maybe he's a little turned and Lady F thinks they are just empty envelopes, but the home help said she knows they had something in them, the home help does, because she felt them. She didn't take one, though. No, home helps have to be honest about other people's property.

Anyway, Lizzie dear, it's shaken us up a bit. He doesn't look much like a pornographer, though. Not that I'd know, of course. At least he hasn't palled up with that George Griffiths. You'll never believe it but George's latest thing is to go on and on about me stealing his things. Well, of course I do, Lizzie, but so would you under the circumstances. He makes everyone's life here a misery.

And this comes with many good wishes to you and your family. I was sorry to hear about Brian needing spectacles. Has Laurie thought about getting some made the next time Brian goes to see his father in Ireland? Graham and I got some lovely cut-glass tumblers there when we were on holiday once. Even Graham used to admit that the Irish are very good with glass and you know how fussy he could be. Maybe Ireland would be a nice place for our next trip, although the sea can get awful rough. I am sorry Laurie has heard bad things about Swanage, and beach parties all night might not exactly be what we're after. I'm not sure I agree with her that teenagers seem to spoil things these days because of course they are only having a bit of fun. Perhaps we could go and join them, Lizzie. What do you think?

Yours aye,

Flo

17. LETTER FROM MARTIN MORRIS TO MO GRIFFITHS

Dear Mo,

I shouldn't have done it. I'm not daft. Of course I know I shouldn't have done it, but it was only going to be the once.

George was downstairs. I was on my way down myself to make a cup of tea when I heard him in the hallway, making some pronouncement about these pictures they have up on the walls in here. You know the sort. One is a box full of different knots, another is a whole lot of clay pipes with dates underneath. They're supposed to stimulate us, although it just makes me think we're in the museum too. They'll be pinning us up soon. *Martin Morris 2008.* I could hear Helen Elliott trying to get a word in edgeways but George wouldn't let her.

I hesitated at the landing just to catch my breath. But then I noticed I was leaning up against George's door and before I knew it, I'd opened it and was taking a look inside.

His room is much bigger than mine, but I was told when I came that I had the smallest room in the house. It suits me just fine. And if mine is empty like a monk's cell, his is just as tidy. Everything in order, shipshape and Bristol-fashion. Remember you saying that once and me laughing at you? I wonder now if it was because that's how you had to be around him. You were always such a messy thing when you were with me. I was just thinking I couldn't see you in this room when I spotted your photograph on the bookcase.

Talk about a moth to a flame. I couldn't let that go, could I? So I took a few steps inside, but then I heard the door shut behind me so I knew I was done in. What could I say if he caught me inside?

Still, I picked up your photograph. You were on some beach. Your hair, your glorious blond hair, was tied up in a scarf but you were laughing. And I looked at your hands and they weren't clenched but they were wide open as if you were about to catch a ball or something. Perhaps it was one of the children you were playing with? George was standing behind you and he was smiling too. But not at the camera. At you.

I put it back quickly. I had been going to take it but it felt wrong now that George was in the shot too. I was hungry for something, though. Suddenly it seemed you were everywhere in the room now, and I needed to have a bit of you. I put my hand out and took the first thing I touched. It was a packet of seeds. I popped them in my pocket and left. My heart was thumping, but when I got outside, I could hear George still droning on and on downstairs.

But then I heard a noise and when I looked around, the door to the room opposite was just shutting. Annabel Armstrong. If it had to be anyone it was a good thing it was her. Her mind's going so no one would believe her word over mine. I rushed back to my room, my heart beating, and then I sat on my bed and looked at the seeds. Cornflowers.

I'll plant them in the spring. And I'll think of you when I do so. You laughing. I didn't see too much of that. We should have laughed more. All the things they robbed us of.

M

18. NOTE FROM GEORGE GRIFFITHS TO FLORENCE OLIVER

Dear Mrs. Oliver,

I know you have been in my room. When I came back on Thursday, I could distinctly smell your cologne and a picture had been knocked over. I have informed the authorities.

George Griffiths

19. LETTER FROM BRENDA LEWIS TO NELL BAKER

Dear Nell,

Thank you for your letter. I am sorry that your father has made claims about other residents to you, and I would indeed appreciate the opportunity for the two of us to work out a way of coming to an amicable solution. However, I am glad that you have managed to dissuade him from any unnecessary instigation of police proceedings.

Please be assured that discretion is a given because, as you know, we put the well-being of our residents above all else. I shall look forward to seeing you on Thursday 26, at 2 p.m., while your father is away from Pilgrim House at his weekly chiropodist appointment.

In the meantime, can I reassure you that no one goes into his room apart from my staff. I appreciate that you do not make any direct accusations of theft, but you will understand that every time your father has brought this matter up, we have carried out thorough checks and nothing of any substance has been missing.

Yours sincerely,
Brenda Lewis

20. LETTER FROM MRS. FISHWICK,

BURTON COMPREHENSIVE SCHOOL, TO NELL BAKER

Dear Ms. Baker,

I have tried several times to call you so I would be grateful if you could ring to make an appointment to discuss Robyn's progress at school. Her teachers have expressed a number of concerns, and it feels that now would be a good time to talk about the best way she can cope as she thinks about a university education. I have checked our school records and we do not have the details for Robyn's father on file. I would be grateful if you could forward these to us if at all possible. We often find that it helps to have both parents present.

I look forward to meeting with you, but in the meantime please do call with any immediate concerns you may have.

Yours sincerely,
Bette Fishwick

21. EMAIL FROM NELL BAKER TO ANGIE GRIFFITHS

Angie,

Why do you never answer your phone? Now I've got problems with Robyn. Apparently her teachers reckon she's not "applying herself to her full abilities." Well, hello, who is? We've had to sign a contract with the school that she would work harder. Can you believe it? And it seems Dad's been upsetting the other residents. Again.

Knock, knock, this is your family calling. Dad needs you.

Nell

22. LETTER FROM CLAUDE BICHOURIE TO ANGELA GRIFFITHS

Chérie,

They say diamonds are a girl's best friend, so may this necklace decorate your neck where I would like to kiss you this weekend. Do not be cross with me for going away. You know I have to spend time with my family.

You are so beautiful, Angela. I did not mean harm by saying you are looking more womanly than usual. It suits you. When you are by my side, I am the proudest man in Paris. I wish we could shout our love from the rooftops, but in the meantime, my diamonds will have to glitter for me.

Claude

23. NOTE LEFT ON KITCHEN TABLE FROM NELL TO ROBYN BAKER

ROBYN,

I HAVE HAD ENOUGH.

1. TIDY YOUR ROOM.
2. FINISH YOUR ENGLISH ESSAY.
3. GO AND VISIT YOUR GRANDFATHER.

IF I COME BACK FROM WORK AND YOU ARE STILL IN BED, I WILL BAN YOU FROM USING THE COMPUTER, TAKE AWAY YOUR MOBILE PHONE AND STOP YOUR CLOTHES ALLOWANCE FOR A MONTH. I MEAN IT. REMEMBER THAT CONTRACT WE MADE WITH THE SCHOOL. THIS IS YOUR LAST CHANCE.

24. ANSWER PHONE MESSAGE FROM
ANTOINE DUPERT TO ANGELA GRIFFITHS

Angela, this is Antoine. However many times I might say I enjoyed our photographic session, it will never be enough. You are more than a natural model, you are a muse. I can't wait to show you the photographs. They are beautiful. You are beautiful, but the photographs have taken on a life of their own. It's as if the connection between you and me has created something uniquely new, something special, living, breathing. I think they might be the best piece of work I have done. Please come again. Even if nothing else happens between you and me, and how can I not hope for more of that, we owe it to the world to take more photographs together.

Ring me.

25. NOTE FROM ROBYN BAKER
SCRIBBLED ON BOTTOM OF NOTE 23.

ROBYN,
    I HAVE HAD ENOUGH.

1. TIDY YOUR ROOM.
2. FINISH YOUR ENGLISH ESSAY.
3. GO AND VISIT YOUR GRANDFATHER.

IF I COME BACK FROM WORK AND YOU ARE <u>STILL</u> IN BED, I WILL BAN YOU FROM USING THE COMPUTER, TAKE AWAY YOUR MOBILE PHONE AND STOP YOUR CLOTHES ALLOWANCE FOR A MONTH. I MEAN IT. REMEMBER THAT CONTRACT WE MADE WITH THE SCHOOL. THIS IS YOUR LAST CHANCE.

Chill, Mum. It's the weekend. I'll go and see Granddad later. Promise.

Hey, did you know that if you hang over the bed and look at the mirror upside down you see your face as it's going to be in fifty years' time? If you're lucky, and the wind changes, they'll abduct me into the Pilgrims.

Love ya,
Robyn

P.S. We need more milk. There wasn't enough for my cereal this morning.

26. ANSWER PHONE MESSAGE FROM
GEORGE GRIFFITHS TO ANGIE GRIFFITHS

Hello Angie,

This is your father speaking at four thirty on Saturday afternoon. I am most distressed. Robyn stopped by and she has had her tongue pierced. Apparently Nell knows, which renders me even more speechless. I told her to go to the bathroom and take it out straightaway, but she informed me she couldn't for fear of infection.

In addition, I have no idea why Robyn came. Even when we talked about her progress at school, she had little to say. And the silly way she dresses makes the other residents feel uncomfortable. I cannot imagine why Nell lets her get away with it. I know Nell would welcome your advice, particularly as I am sure she looks up to you. Apart from this, I am as well as can be expected.

Thank you for your recent postcard of Euro Disney. I am most surprised that it is doing well as I would never have thought the French and roller coasters were a good mix. Both are far too excitable.

This has been your father.

27. LETTER FROM MARTIN MORRIS TO MO GRIFFITHS

Hello Mo,

Well, I said I would tell you about Robyn when I had some news. She came today to visit George, and I made sure I had the chance to talk to her after. She was a bit upset, to tell you the truth. Things hadn't gone too well with her grandfather and she was hunting around the reception looking for tissues. I took her into the yard for a bit and we sat on the bench near the apple tree until she felt better. I could feel the packet of seeds I'd taken from George's room in my pocket. I like to carry them around with me.

I think you'd like her, Mo. In fact, I'm sure you would. She's got a bit of your fire about her, once you get past the prickles. But then you had those too, didn't you? I could never get it right with you. You were always leaving before you even arrived. Like you were just waiting for me to do something wrong so you could tell me you were skipping out.

But hark at me. I always did get it wrong, didn't I, angel? Anyway, let me try to describe Robyn in a way that will satisfy you. She's about your height, tall enough to look into my eyes, and she looks direct. I'll say that for her. She meets life head-on. Her hair is all over the place, though. And dyed crow-black. She's got a white face, looks as if she's ill but it's only makeup, and when she laughs, Mo, she puts her hand up to her mouth as if she's trying to hold the laughter in to keep it for herself.

I talked to her about art and poetry because I guessed not many others would think to do that. I didn't mention you, of course, but it felt right it should be me passing on the names of some of your precious nature poets. Clare, Thoreau, Whitman. You see they're engraved on my heart. She said she wanted to go and live on a farm up in Scotland. Her dad's Scottish apparently. "I'd be on my own," she said. "I want to live really simply and naturally. Get back to nature."

"How interesting," I lied. Then I asked if she wouldn't be lonely. "Oh no," she said. "I'm used to that."

When she picked up her bag, I noticed it had this sign painted on it in big pink letters. I Hate Life.

"You don't really," I asked her. I wanted to scoop her up and look after her forevermore. It was just like I always felt with you. But then, just like you used to, she surprised me.

"No," she said, putting her hand up to her mouth again to hide her laugh in that way of hers. "But it pisses the teachers off."

See what I mean? Apart from the language, she's got a spark about her that you can't help but warm to. I went to see her off from reception and as I was coming back, I saw George sitting in the lounge reading the paper. I stood and stared at him. I'm not ashamed to say I could feel my blood rise up then. He has no idea how much he has.

I have to do something, Mo. I can't sit back and let him bully them all like this. Not our girls.

M

28. EMAIL FROM NELL BAKER TO ANGIE GRIFFITHS

Hey Angie,

I can't believe you're finally coming over. Dad'll be pleased as he'll be able to complain firsthand about Robyn's piercings. I did wonder what he'd think about it but he hasn't said anything to me. Mind you, he seemed to help her the other day. She hasn't said anything, but when she came back from visiting him—of course I had to make her—she'd only been to the library to get out some books of poetry. I asked if they were a school thing but she said no, and when I looked at them I saw they were all the poets Mum liked.

Do you remember Dad ever reading anything apart from the business pages and his accountancy journals? I've been racking my brains but I guess he must have taken more notice of Mum than we gave him credit for. She loved poetry so much, didn't she? I picked up one of the books last night when Robyn had gone to bed, and it made me cry.

Oh, Angie, it will be so nice to have you here. You haven't been back since the funeral, and that was nearly three years ago. I'd love to talk about Mum. You were always so much closer to her when we were growing up. Do you think she was ever really happy? I don't know why but when I was thinking about her last night, I thought perhaps she wasn't. Of course you disappearing made her unhappy but I mean before that too. She was never quite there, was she? She'd always be looking out of the window as if she could see something out there we couldn't.

Was that what made you go? The way she always kept us close, worrying if we were safe or not. It's a mistake I'm not going to make with Robyn anyway. She needs to make up her own mind about things, even if her decisions don't always seem like the most sensible ones.

29. LETTER FROM MARTIN MORRIS TO MO GRIFFITHS

Dear Mo,

I had another little visit from Robyn yesterday. I was in the lounge when she walked into reception. I thought she was visiting George, but she was looking around a bit nervous like, and then when she spotted me, she came straight over to where I was sitting.

She didn't bother to say hello. "Those poems were OK," she said, and I could see her bag was bulging with library books. "Tell me more."

I guess it's just her manner to be gruff so I racked my brains. I told her all the other names I could remember from our conversations and the books I used to see you reading later in the park. She wrote it all down in this little notebook she has, as serious as could be. I said she should look at the paintings of Turner. "See how he does light," I told her. I was thinking about how we used to watch the sky from the studio window, and I got you that book of Turner's watercolors as a present. We used to pore over it together until you told me that these were the kind of photographs I should take. Maybe I should have listened to you because then you might have stayed with me and everything would have been different, but I loved my photography. It wasn't bad to me, Mo. Nothing bad about a woman's body.

The other thing I told her to read was Thomas Hardy. See, I've never forgotten coming back to the studio one day when I'd arranged to meet you there. I always liked to make an excuse to be out when you came so I could find you waiting for me. This time, you were sitting in the chair by the window and I thought I'd surprise you so I took my shoes off and started to creep across the floor. I stopped when I saw that you were crying, but not before I had time to notice the book on your knee. *The Mayor of Casterbridge*. I read it after when you'd gone back to George, and I wept too. But not as much as you did. I never told you I'd found you like that, Mo. I just crept back out and came back five minutes later, all bustling and shouting. It annoyed you, I expect, but at least you didn't have any tears left in your eyes and you never mentioned the crying. I didn't ask, because I didn't want you to tell me it wasn't just about the book.

Anyway, young Robyn looks as if she's got lots of crying left inside her, and if there's one thing I've learned from women over the years, it's that they need to get it out somehow. She didn't see George. I asked if she was going to and she looked a bit sheepish and said maybe next time.

Perhaps I shouldn't have felt so pleased about that. I couldn't stop smiling even when Mrs. Oliver came over and propositioned me. Don't get jealous, Mo. We're too old for all that in here. You and I, though, we will never get too old. I suppose we have that, at least.

M

30. LETTER FROM GEORGE GRIFFITHS TO BRENDA LEWIS

Dear Mrs. Lewis,

While I am certainly appreciative of your attempts to entertain us, I wonder if you thought last night's speaker was totally appropriate for the audience. The Welsh voice in flow is indeed a wonderful thing, but thirty minutes of dubious rugby songs from a milkman left much to be desired. I am only grateful Catherine Francis misunderstood several of the words and thought they were religious.

In addition, I cannot have been the only one woken up early this morning by Annabel Armstrong chanting a refrain from one of the more unsuitable songs from last night. It seems we have become a laughingstock.

Some people, I am afraid, do not understand common civility and it is a shame when we let them into our homes.

If you would like me to take over the running of the social events, I would be happy to oblige.

Yours sincerely,
George Griffiths

31. LETTER FROM FLORENCE OLIVER TO LIZZIE CORN

Dear Lizzie,

Well, I did it! Exactly as you suggested!

Remember how Graham always said you were a bad influence on me? Oh, I laughed and laughed when I read in your letter about asking Martin to take my picture. I know you just meant it as a bit of fun but I was feeling mischievous. After all, I'm seventy-nine, what have I got to lose? I told myself that if he looked horrified, I was just going to pretend I was joking. I got him when he was in one of those armchairs in the sitting room. They have low seats, those ones, so I knew he wouldn't be able to get out fast. He was looking happy too, otherwise I might have lost my nerve. I kept reminding myself how he said I looked beautiful.

"Martin Morris," I said, "will you take some of your photos of me?" You should have seen his face. He stopped smiling and looked as if he'd been hit by a tankful smack in the chops, but then he got weaselly. I remember that look from my Graham. I could see him thinking. What's in it for me here?

"You're very lovely," he said, but mechanical, not like when he complimented me before. His eyes were all screwed up and he wasn't really looking at me, which was a shame because I'd got dressed up. I'd put on some makeup and had my hair done nicely by one of the Tuesday hairdressing girls, and I was wearing that flowery dress too. You know that one I wore when we went to the bandstand at Margate and you said it made me look slim. Helen Elliott always gets a bit bilious anyway, but she gave me such a glare when I came into the sitting room that I knew I was looking good.

"You're very lovely." That's all he said. I smiled back at him but I was a bit disappointed. It didn't have the same impact second time around, and I thought he'll have to do better than that if he's to get me relaxed enough for some proper sweetheart photos. I was regretting it more than a bit, I don't mind telling you, and I was all set to have a laugh about it when he surprised me.

"So what do I get in exchange?" he said, and he winked.

I knew he'd wake us up. I feel like Prince Charming has cut down the thorns and some color has come back into our lives.

"That depends," I told him. "I'm a respectable woman."

He smiled at that in a way that, between you and me, made my cheeks go hot. And then he said he'd got some kind of plan and he wanted an intelligent woman to help him. He didn't want to tell me about it straightaway but, Lizzie, don't you fear, I'll write to you the minute I know everything. I need to catch the mail with this now anyway.

This is better than Blackpool, my darling girl. For once I don't feel jealous of you with your family and all the excitement over Laurie's new man. I agree that a diamond earring is worrying on a man and the name is very odd. Troy. But Susan Reed says that lots of people meet in supermarkets. Her niece works in one, and apparently in the evenings, the frozen food aisle is always busy with men and women getting more excited than they should over broccoli. You have to look for the ones getting single portions, apparently. I wonder what Graham and Frank would have made of that.

And what did you say Troy was? A massager? I didn't know men could do that.

Oh, but what do you think Martin has in mind? "I'm a respectable woman," that's what I told him. "Are you?" he said straight off. "You look like a bit of a minx to me." And he raised an eyebrow. Remember how your Frank used to do that and how you told me once it always gave you a bit of a tingle. I don't mind telling you that, although I laughed and laughed, I got a bit of a tingle too. A minx. Me. If only Graham could have heard him. Well, I suppose it was a good job Graham didn't hear him really but I feel twenty-two all over again. It's just like you and me at the Palace ballroom and all the fun we had there. They say you're only as old as you feel and Martin's quite a bit younger than anyone else in here.

"My husband was an army boxer," I told him. I know it's a lie but Graham had the physique for it, didn't he? I'm sure he could have boxed if he wanted.

"Yes, but he's not here, is he?" Martin said. "It's just you and me and I don't think you'll be giving me a bloody nose."

Just you and me! I wonder what's in those envelopes, though. The ones the home help told us about that were never sent. I like a man with a secret, mind.

Yours aye,
Flo

P.S. I think Laurie might be wrong about Ireland being too expensive. Susan Reed has a second cousin living there so she's going to look into coach tours for us. I know you said you would never do another after Blackpool but we can make sure we get one with proper toilets this time. And seats downstairs.

P.P.S. OK, I'm seventy-nine plus a few, but I intend to wait a few more years for my eightieth birthday if it's all the same to you. How did two girls as young as us get so old?

32. ANSWER PHONE MESSAGE FROM
   ### GEORGE GRIFFITHS TO ANGIE GRIFFITHS

Hello Angie, this is your father speaking to you. Speaking to your machine I should say, but it's your father here. It's three thirty-five on Tuesday afternoon. I hope you are feeling well. I was relieved to hear from Nell that you are planning to visit us as I fear things are not going too well for her. Nell does her best but Robyn has turned into a complete rebel. She has been lying to her mother.

I found out by accident when Nell thanked me for helping her with her schoolwork.

"I haven't," I said, straight off, and you should have seen Nell's face go white. I dread to think what other fibs that girl has been telling her mother.

I have promised to draw up a schedule for Robyn. It always used to help you and Nell to have some focus. Focus and discipline, I've found, are the tricks to succeeding in most things. I myself am having to apply it to my own life due to petty annoyances here with other residents at Pilgrim House. Anyway, thank you for the card of Notre Dame, although you would think they would be able to take a photograph without all the scaffolding. Yes, I do understand that it is not always possible for you to get to the phone, and I appreciate the efforts you make to keep in touch. I will leave you now. It's three forty-two.

And this has been your father.

33. LETTER FROM MARTIN MORRIS TO MO GRIFFITHS

Dear Mo,

Do you remember how jealous you used to get?

There was never any need but I think you knew that. And you liked it too, didn't you? You told me once it made you feel alive. You were always such a strange little thing.

So shall I tell you about the women I'm living with here and make you jealous? Would you like that, darling? What I wouldn't give to make you feel alive.

First off, there's Catherine Francis. Lady F, Mrs. Oliver calls her for no reason I can see other than Catherine wears pink lipstick and silk scarves tied around her neck like the Queen. She doesn't speak much to me. I thought at first that George had his eye on her, but now I'm not sure. He told her off the other day for half finishing the crossword in the paper. I think he was angry she got more clues than he normally manages.

Helen Elliott wants to be Catherine's friend so badly that it can only annoy Catherine. Every Friday when Catherine makes her special bus trip into town for an afternoon shopping, Helen does everything she can to be invited too. She even hangs around the lobby looking at the pictures but Catherine always sweeps by her. Nice enough, but firm. Mrs. Oliver can't understand why Helen doesn't just go into town on her own, but of course it's not the shopping Helen wants, but Catherine. Well, I know all about that kind of wanting.

Then there's Susan Reed. She has a large family and you probably don't need to know any more than that. Oh, and that they visit. Often. She's always after George to get his, your, grandchild and hers together, but they're not really Robyn's type. All side parts and stamp collections.

Annabel Armstrong is next. Between you and me, she's well meaning but a bit off her rocker. None of the rest of us say anything but I've noticed we all do our best to hide her excesses. Ever since she caught me coming out of George's room that time she's taken to calling me a thief. It gets annoying but I've managed to turn it into a joke because as the other residents agree, there are far far worse places you can go than here. We wouldn't want that for anyone, even Annabel.

It's hard to separate Beth Crosbie from her husband, and you wouldn't want to. BethandKeith, we call them. Keith's not a proper resident, as George keeps pointing out to anyone who will listen. Mind, Keith seems to go out of his way to drive George mad. The other day he even asked him if he'd mind moving to a different armchair so he could sit next to Beth to watch some television program about dogs. George went straight to his room to write one of his famous letters to Brenda, I expect.

Mrs. Oliver is the one I understand best. "Call me Florence," she said the other day. "Not bloody likely," I replied. "Before I know it, you'll be strapping me to a bed and shoving thermometers where I don't want them like Florence bloody Nightingale." She laughed then. In fact, she reminds me of your Trisha. The way they both liked a joke. What happened to her, I wonder? She came back to the studio that day just to have some more photographs taken, Mo. I wish you believed me. Nothing more than that.

God knows, I wasn't a saint. But never with someone you cared about. And then later never with someone I cared about. But that's a different story.

So there you have it, your competition. Odd lot we are here. And of course there's George. But you know all about him. Too well, I should think.

And now, until later.

M

34. NOTE FROM GEORGE GRIFFITHS TO BRENDA LEWIS

Dear Mrs. Lewis,

You asked me to make a list specifically of the issues that are concerning me so I have outlined these below.

First of all, the following things have gone missing from my room. They are not in the chronological order of their disappearance but include:

Two bars of opened soap
One tube of toothpaste—Colgate
A postcard from my daughter in France
A pencil, just sharpened
A copy of the Daily Telegraph, with a half-completed crossword, dated 21 February
A packet of seeds

I appreciate that none of these are of monetary worth. However, the thieving is of grave concern to me, particularly as I have my suspicions.

Second, I would like to express my concern about Annabel Armstrong's health. My understanding is that one of the conditions of residency in Pilgrim House is the ability to care for yourself. However, it is becoming increasingly clear that Mrs. Armstrong is unable to take responsibility for her personal grooming and this combined with her continual chanting of obscenities makes me wonder if it would be kinder to find her accommodation where she could receive more support.

Third, while I appreciate that a husband and wife will want to be together, please could you confirm that Keith Crosbie makes a financial contribution to the running of Pilgrim House? We are, after all, a charity and yet I have noticed he enjoys several cups of tea during the time he is here and often takes a biscuit. When I questioned him about it, he said he was merely using up Beth's share. In the appropriate circumstances, I am not unsympathetic to Beth's lack of appetite, but a husband using it to further his own greed seems a bit much. If you think it might help your case, I am happy to do a spreadsheet of a typical resident's consumption and arrange some kind of chart in the kitchen whereby we all keep a note of what we take.

And last, I was shocked to see tattoos on the hand of the new staff member. I realize we have to move with the times, and I have nothing against people defiling their bodies should they choose to do so in the privacy of their own home. However, it might be more suitable if you could advise him to keep his marks covered while he is at work. I know that Catherine Francis, in particular, is not used to such things. Perhaps he could wear gloves?

I look forward to hearing your plan of action.

Yours sincerely,
George Griffiths

35. LETTER FROM FLORENCE OLIVER TO LIZZIE CORN

Dear Lizzie,

I was only joking when I said you made me do the photographs, and I'm sorry you took it so badly because no slur was intended. Anyway, I am flummoxed you thought I was blaming you for that unfortunate incident with the officers at Aldershot. Truth is, I'd forgotten about dancing with the young lieutenant, although it's true that Graham did think you were involved and it was wrong of me not to stand up for you more at the time. All I meant was that we egg each other on, love. We both know it's all just a bit of fun.

I know you mean to be kind by worrying about me but I'm really not making a fool of myself. Yes, I do realize how old I am.

Write soon, Lizzie, and tell me all is forgiven. I shall wait for the mail.

Yours aye,
Flo

P.S. And he was heavenly, that officer in Aldershot. He kissed my hand, you know, and just gently licked my thumbnail until I thought I might have to faint. You wouldn't have caught Graham doing anything like that. Truth is, I was grateful to you.

36. LETTER FROM MARTIN MORRIS TO MO GRIFFITHS

Dear Mo,

Although every day I feel I'm getting closer to your family, there are still times when I wish I'd never left my studio. I preferred it when I could think of George as some kind of perfect hero, taking you away from me. Honestly, love, he has to be the coldest fish I've ever met. I don't mean to speak ill of your husband, but everything is about the right way to behave with him.

Just yesterday, I came down to find Helen Elliott in the kitchen in tears. "What's up?" I asked her, and she refused to tell me at first. Then she admitted that George had told her to stop bothering Catherine Francis. "I am mortified," she kept saying, and it took at least two cups of tea before I could get her to stop crying. George has only put this chart up in the kitchen, by the way, which we're supposed to check off every time we use a tea bag. No one does so I bet he has already written to poor Brenda to complain.

The long and the short of it is that we both went to see Catherine Francis because Helen wanted to apologize. "Do you think it best?" she kept asking me. I didn't but I've learned enough about women to know that once they have determined something in their mind then nothing will make them change it. And of course, Catherine was flummoxed. She hadn't said anything to George. "Did he really say you were bothering me?" she asked.

Helen fluttered a bit. "He said it might be construed that way," she said, and I thought "you're lying, miss," but I wasn't going to spoil the moment. I was enjoying being publicly indignant about George too much.

"But why did you never say you wanted to come for tea with me?" Catherine was as nice as anything. "It will be lovely to have company."

"Really? How lovely," Helen fluttered.

"Lovely," I said, joining in with enthusiasm. "Isn't this lovely?" But neither of them took any notice of me.

And so they're going together next Friday. Catherine's just shy, of course, and sometimes that can be taken the wrong way. I don't know if you remember me telling you about Sue. She was the model from Hastings, the one with the red hair. Everyone thought she was hoity-toity, but she just couldn't get the words out at the right time. That was why I always used to photograph her with a cat. She could talk on and on to animals and it would make her seem softer somehow in the pictures.

I wish I'd asked you more about George when I could. It was my stupid pride that stopped me, but information always comes in useful. I can't help wondering if it would have made a difference if I had put up more of a fight for you. Well, maybe it's not too late for something to happen.

M

37. LETTER FROM GEORGE GRIFFITHS TO BRENDA LEWIS

Dear Mrs. Lewis,

In addition to the points raised in my last letter, I would also be grateful if you could show Florence Oliver how to shut doors more quietly. It is not that she exactly slams the door, but if she were to learn to use the handle and pull the door closed with that, then we could all enjoy a more tranquil ambience. Consideration of others is a common courtesy.

I have tried to talk to her myself but to no avail.

Yours sincerely,
George Griffiths

38. LETTER FROM FLORENCE OLIVER TO LIZZIE CORN

Dearest Lizzie,

You and I are friends again!

I read your card with such joy, Lizzie. The moment I saw the picture of those two poor little Royal boys, I knew it was from you and that you had forgiven me. And yes, if you're sure that's what you want, I'll carry on telling you everything that's happening here. I shall smile to think of our letters in a box marked Incontinence Pads. You are right to think Troy won't venture in there.

Trouble is I hardly know where to begin. Oh, I know we've both had our moments over the years but it feels good to be alive. Do you remember that tattoo artist at Southend who tried to persuade you to have a rose on your thigh? I don't mind telling you I was jealous of that but, with the greatest respect, in terms of wickedness, he has nothing on Martin.

So let me tell you about the plan.

I am going to seduce George Griffiths!

What do you think of that?

Of course, I'm not going to seduce him properly. I'm not that daft. Just become close to him. Martin thought of the idea. It's so we can get evidence on him and then we are going to make a complaint. We're going to give him a taste of his own medicine.

It's just a bit of fun so don't you go getting all sour-lemony on me and taking the wind out of my sails. No one who doesn't deserve it will get hurt. George makes everyone's life a misery so this is going to be our revenge. Martin's and mine. Besides, it's not as if there's anything else for us to do in here. We had to sit through a talk yesterday afternoon from a woman who makes bread. She told us how therapeutic it can be to pound and beat the dough. She'd brought some with her already prepared that she kept throwing up and catching until Annabel Armstrong got too excited and the new help, Steve, had to take her out. But I had to leave the room too. I kept thinking about Graham and how red his face used to get when he was angry. He always had to be right. I suppose it was his army training. As I went, I could see Martin giving me a smile. I don't think he'd hurt a fly. It's unusual for a man to be gentle like that.

Mind you, he hasn't mentioned the photographs recently. You'll probably be relieved to hear that, but you were wrong about my reasons for having them done. Graham used to get those magazines, you know. I found them once under the mattress when he was away training, but I never told him I knew because I liked looking at them. Was that wrong of me? It wasn't that they gave me a thrill, or not for the reasons you might be thinking. I just liked to think about those women and how different their lives were from mine. I imagined what it must have been like to get undressed up like that and for no one to laugh at you. The opposite really. Sometimes I'd even do it, when I knew Graham was away and no one would catch me. I'd pose half dressed in front of the mirror. I never blamed Graham for preferring those women to me. Not then.

But suddenly I feel I need to have a quiet lie-down.

Yours aye,

Flo

39. LETTER FROM MARTIN MORRIS TO MO GRIFFITHS

Dear Mo,

I imagined him different. That's the truth. But when I'm with him now, do you know what the worst bit is? I think of you. Because I can't forget, Mo, and I don't believe you could either. So when I'm in the same room as him, I think of what it must have been like for you. I wonder whether maybe you sat with him like I did last night and if you couldn't bear to look at him either. And if all you could think of was me. Did you think of me when you were talking to him, Mo? When you cooked his dinner, did you think of the time I dressed you up in an apron and the yellow scarf around your head and said I was going to take your photo just like the perfect housewife? It was supposed to make you laugh, but it didn't. Of course, it didn't. It wasn't bloody funny, was it?

But you can't blame me for being angry. You can't blame me for that. It was a wicked lie that you thought I would have harmed you. Remember that time when I begged you to come to the studio, and you said it was going to be the last time because it scared you when I got so intense.

If it scared you, what about me? After you'd left the studio that day, all I can remember is curling up in a ball and crying. The tears were still trying to get through even after they were all used up, but I couldn't seem to let my body know that it was empty.

A model called Heather found me the next morning. I'd told her to come in early because she had to go to the dentist later and after she'd got no reply, she tested the door, found it open and came up the stairs. They kept saying in the hospital that she'd saved my life and that I was ungrateful for turning my head away when she came to visit.

I kept calling out your name but no one knew who you were. I'd never said anything, you see, not even when I thought we were going to be together forever. You'd made me promise to be discreet. Heather even asked some of the other girls but they didn't think there was a model called Mo. Eventually they came to the conclusion that I must have been calling for Mahad and got him to come and pick me up. I wrote the first letter to you after I came out of the hospital. You wrote back at first, didn't you, two or three times, but then you begged me to stop. Trouble was that by then nothing could stop me writing to you, but I still kept my promise. I didn't mail any of them. Well, just the one.

I should have sent you them all. I wish I had bombarded you with my love. I wish I'd stormed around there and rescued you instead of just watching at a distance. As if you ever really thought I could harm you. So this is my plan. I am going to finally take your girls for my own just as I know you would have wanted. I am going to rescue them from George. All of them. Nell and Robyn, and even Angie in France. I am going to make them all safe.

Florence Oliver is going to help me, not that she knows exactly what her involvement is going to be. You see, when I was taking photographs there was a certain type of woman who would always say they never wanted anyone to see their pictures. I could tell them a mile off. I don't know if I told you about this way I had of choosing my models. I'd go to clubs and leave some of my magazines lying about, and then I'd just hang around until a woman came over and picked one up. She'd circle for a bit maybe, but she wouldn't be able to resist. And that's when I'd start speaking to her. It never failed. Mrs. Oliver has that same spark about her as those women had. There's a desperate need in her to be noticed, however much she might resist. She won't mind me using her photographs.

I remember you saying once that George would always be covering your body up, not from jealousy but correctness. You see where I'm going, Mo. If George gets fond of Florence and he finds out I have photographs of her, then he will hate it. I will have the final victory over all his rules and right behavior.

It will take a will of steel and a cold heart. But I'm learning. After fifty bloody years of just watching and waiting, it's time for some action.

M

40. LETTER FROM NELL BAKER TO BRENDA LEWIS

Dear Brenda,

Thanks for such a helpful meeting yesterday. I am sorry that my father has caused you so much inconvenience. As you suggest, I will do everything I can to encourage him to enter more fully into the social life of Pilgrim House and to develop some more interests. I can see that more occupations will be healthy for him.

In the meantime, I am enclosing a small donation to the staff social fund. I hope that you will be able to use it as a way of saying thank you for looking after my father so well.

I was also grateful to have the chance to talk to Steve Jenkins. He is, as you said, an asset to the home, particularly with his experience of personal training and his charitable volunteering. I will consider his suggestion of coming in to talk about my work but will have to think first of an angle that might be interesting to the residents. My father finds my job as a trend forecaster hard to understand, but I would very much like to give something back for all the kindness you have shown my family.

With best wishes,
Yours sincerely,
Nell Baker

41. EMAIL FROM NELL BAKER TO ANGIE GRIFFITHS

Brenda suggested we persuade Dad to take up some hobbies. Any ideas? I was wondering about forced marches and double-column accounting. "Does he have any friends who might like to visit him?" she asked. I was about to say something sarcastic about whether she could imagine anyone wanting to visit Dad, but then I couldn't do it. "He has his family," I said. She gave me a funny look then, but it's probably because she knew I was protecting him. Why do we always do that?

I wonder if it's because people normally just see the one side of him, but it's easy to forget how we used to go to him when we were in trouble. Mum was for the good times but you could always rely on Dad to sort things out, couldn't you? He'd get out that notepad of his, get you to tell him the facts, turn it into an action list and suddenly things seemed doable.

He's drawn up a work schedule for Robyn. She was furious at first, but when I went into her bedroom I noticed she'd pinned it up by her bed. "Are you going to follow it?" I asked. It's fairly ridiculous. Up at six every morning, bed at eight thirty. You can imagine. "No," she said, "but it's so granddad, isn't it?"

She was right. It was. He drives us all mad, but I could still see the comfort for her in having a chart like that to look at.

42. LETTER FROM FLORENCE OLIVER TO LIZZIE CORN

Dear Lizzie,

I am wiped out. Shattered. Susan Reed had her family around again today. They were allowed to have their dinner with us and you should have heard the shouting. I like a bit of life, as you know, but it made my head hurt. No one said anything, not even when the smallest boy started throwing his mashed potato around.

When I went into the dining room to look for Martin later, Sophi and Steve were wiping all the mess from the walls. "If it's not one end of the age scale causing trouble, it's the other," Sophi said, when she saw me standing there. She's come in for work experience before she goes to university. Uni, they call it now, just as she's called Sophi. "What happened to the e?" I asked her once. "E's too much trouble," she said, and she drew me a picture of her name with a smiley face over the i. She's a lively girl, although not particularly favored in the looks department. Unlike Steve. He's a tonic.

I couldn't help thinking of you during dinner. Not about the kids, I'm sure Brian and Amy are much better behaved, but you and me. We were such mice, weren't we? Remember when we first met and we'd sit together at those army dinners when the men would get drunk and start playing silly buggers. We spent such a long time just smiling at each other, but then once we got talking we couldn't stop. Maybe that's what Graham and Frank were scared of, us spilling the beans about them. Divide and rule, and all that. It would be about the only bloody thing they were scared of.

Anyway, that's all oil under the bridge. I went to the sitting room after our noisy lunch because I thought I'd sit down quietly for a bit, and Helen Elliott came up. "We were wondering if you'd like to play Scrabble," she said. I had to think a bit before I got her meaning. Ever since she started going around with Lady F, she clips her words like that poor girl in the hat who got dirt in her eye in that silly train film. I knew Helen only asked me because Martin has been paying me attention. It's the sort of thing other women notice.

"Don't mind if I do," I said.

"Those children made an awful racket, didn't they?" she said as we walked over to where Lady F was sitting.

"I suppose we're used to quiet when we eat our dinner," I said.

"Lunch," she corrected me, but so quickly I knew she couldn't help it. I pretended I hadn't heard her, but when she took her seat next to Lady F and the Scrabble board was all set up, I said I was feeling a little headachy so would they pardon me? And then I came up to my room and started writing this letter. I don't think she meant any harm, Lizzie, but even so, I'm tired of worrying about saying the wrong thing. I don't think I'm even supposed to say pardon anymore but they're all just words, clipped or not.

Now, let's be more cheery. It's nearly spring and I will be with you soon. Do you think Laurie will put the extra bed in your room again? Although it's tight, we're cozy like that, aren't we? Two peas in a pod. Remember last year and we stayed up talking all night. I can't wait to tell you all about Martin. I wonder what you will make of him.

Yours aye,

Flo

43. LETTER FROM MARTIN MORRIS TO MO GRIFFITHS

Dear Mo,

You will be pleased to hear that Robyn and I have quite a little relationship going. She has even started to let me see some of her poems. All the usual stuff about teenage heartbreak and no one understanding her, but I pretend to be interested.

"You should think not just about what's in front of your eyes but what could be lying underneath," I told her. "Look around you here. For instance, look at Annabel. What do you see?" She looked blank, and I told her how Annabel used to be an actress in the West End. How her waist measured only seventeen inches, and she'd lived in a house with four parrots, all of whom had been specially trained by admirers to tell her how beautiful she was every time she came into a room.

"No!" Robyn said.

"Yes," I replied. I enjoyed her reaction. It made me remember how, every time I set up a shot, I would create a story for the model to walk into. Now, I'd tell them, imagine you live on a barge on the River Seine, you've just been feeding your croissant to the ducks and you hear me calling to you. I've been working all day, I'm tired, and you look up at me, concerned and wanting to take my burdens from me. And they'd look at the camera then but they wouldn't see the lens, or me behind it, because they'd be on that boat. It always gave something special to the photograph.

I want to teach Robyn about that. How there's always another world we can step into. A parallel life that's better than the one we live in, just waiting for us. After she'd gone, bug-eyed and keen to come back and have a gape at the beautiful, wasp-waisted Annabel who had so many lovers, I spent some time going through the old photographs I kept. I'd hemmed and hawed about getting rid of them when I came here, a fresh start and all that, but I'm glad now I didn't. Apart from the fact you didn't like it, I'm not ashamed of what I did. I didn't just make women beautiful, I gave us all a glimpse of what we might be.

Sweethearts. That's what I used to call them. A sweetheart shot. You, of course, were my only proper sweetheart shot, the one who went straight to my heart.

Everyone's got photographs here, family members boxed up in frames and displayed on shelves or bedside tables, but mine are fresher. A burst of spring in our winter home. Some are just contact prints, only a few marked with red stars. I've been trying to work out how I picked the best ones because they all look perfect now. I guess I could afford to be choosy then.

Then. Hard to remember it was real. My photography and you. But I couldn't have both, could I? And then I didn't have either. It hurts to look at the photographs from the end, when I was drinking so heavily. I was never sure if I had put film in the camera or not. Better to stop when I did. I was lucky Mahad let me stay on in the studio and gave me work in the newsagent's. Of course, he knew what I'd been through firsthand. It makes a difference.

All it takes now is a long deep look to remember the girls. Sue, Heather, Pauline, Jackie, Helen, Jenny. I didn't get close to all of them, but I can't help feeling soft inside when I look now. They make me feel alive. A world I can step inside.

And I got out of the business at the right time too. Wrong reasons, right time. When I think of what I saw in some of those magazines I had to stack up on the top shelf, it's hard to think mine were considered daring once. All the photographers I knew working at the same time as me treated the girls with respect. Sam Davies, over in Bromley, even married one of them and carried on using her in his magazine. A nice girl. I had hopes once that the two of you might become friends, the four of us going out together and doing all the normal stuff I knew you liked.

It was Sam who got me into the collectors' market, right

after you left. I think he felt sorry for me. It used to make me breathless how much money would change hands for those commissions, especially when I was asked for something particular. A favorite girl, maybe, in a special pose. The rules were always the same: only one picture printed, and the negative burned. I valued my life too much to disobey this, I'm not joking, but I'd always sneak a different pose of the girl during a session for my files. I planned on calling it a test shot if anyone had ever queried it.

I had my own rules too. All the girls had to be of legal age, to be there of their own free will, and to agree to what they were being photographed doing. Oh, and I refused to let the client sit in on the shot. This was the rule that caused the most fuss, but it was the one I insisted on. I was producing a piece of art, not a peep show, and it meant that me, the girl, and the client all retained a certain respect for each other. Sometimes that respect was the only thing I had going for me.

That, and the girls, of course. I can tell you now that I had my choice. God knows why, but after a day in the studio, they seemed to want me. Normally I picked the girls who had caught the eye of the richest collectors. Not because they were the most beautiful, there were some very different tastes out there, but because I would always know that, in this one thing at least, I was getting the real thing, while the client just got my idea of the girl. But even then, you were never far from my thoughts. In the morning, I couldn't wait to get rid of them. I always kept the photographs, though.

Why am I telling you all this now? I want you to know everything about me. Everything out in the air, open and clean. Although from what I'm learning about your family, I'm not the only one who has been living in the shadows.

M

44. EMAIL FROM NELL BAKER TO ANGIE GRIFFITHS

Hey Angie,

You've got to laugh at Dad sometimes. He's now got it into his head that I need to get back together with James. "That girl needs a father," he said about Robyn. "She's got one," I said, "and it's her right to choose not to see him." He snorted then. Actually snorted and said, "in my day." We all know about his day when a man like James who, what does Dad call it, bats for the other side, would have to carry on living with me and making us all miserable.

But tell me this, did you ever think there was something askew in our family? Even when we were all together, we still felt out of balance. It doesn't seem like that for Robyn and me. And didn't even when it was Robyn, James, and me. But when I look back at our photographs, or try to remember events from childhood, it's always as if there's something missing. Either missing, or too much, I'm not sure.

Still, I would like to find someone one day. For companionship as much as anything. But I don't fancy Mark, thank you very much. Of course I know the old joke about men and uniforms, but I'm not sure a nylon security jacket is exactly the stuff of dreams. Plus I can't see how he is guarding anything when he seems to have taken it upon himself to stand by the door of the building every time I come in and out. After your stupid flower delivery, he thinks it's funny to wink at me continuously.

What about you, Angie? Have you met someone properly available or are you still tied up with that married Frenchman? We haven't done all that well for ourselves, have we? The fabulous Griffiths girls. Could that be anything to do with our beloved father, do you think? Maybe we should find him a girlfriend. Now *that* would be a miracle.

Nell

45. ANSWER PHONE MESSAGE FROM
GEORGE GRIFFITHS TO ANGIE GRIFFITHS

Angie, this is your father, George Griffiths here. Leaving another message on your telephone. I have left several, Angie. It's Wednesday, 10:07 a.m. If you don't get this message, I would be grateful if you could let him, me, your father, know. You can't trust machines. I've told you that before. Anyway, I hope work is going well, Angie. Do get in touch if I can be of any help. So I'll leave you now. I know you're busy but I'd be grateful if you could give your sister a ring. She misses you. Thank you for your latest card. In my opinion, Monet's gardens look as if they need a good prune, but I can see your mother would have liked the color. It's 10:10 a.m. now, Angie, and your father wishes you a good day.

46. EMAIL FROM NELL BAKER TO ANGIE GRIFFITHS

I am so not turning into Dad. It's just common sense that if someone has a job, especially as a security guard, then they should do it. The devil makes work for idle hands etc. etc. Mark never seems to do anything useful, and the other day when I asked him if he could spare the time to carry up some boxes to my office, he jumped at the chance.

OK, OK, I do see what you mean. So how come you get to be Mum, all mysterious but with everyone loving her, while I get to be Dad?

I had another go at Robyn about seeing James this week but she's still refusing. Stubborn, like someone else in the family we could mention. But I was wondering if you ever wished you'd been pushed to see Mum after you'd left? She got so quiet at the end without you. Dad kept bustling around making more and more plans, and rules, and schedules for the two of them until I thought he might burst. It was his way of coping, of course, but she gave up. As if just keeping going was too much of an ef-

fort. It was almost as if she'd lost a battle with someone. I often wondered
whether it was because she didn't have you anymore.

47. LETTER FROM GEORGE GRIFFITHS TO BRENDA LEWIS

Dear Brenda,

I am still awaiting a response from you to my letter of 17 February. In the meantime, I have taken the liberty of drafting a rec-
ommendation sheet of when residents can invite family and
friends to avoid inconveniencing others. As you will see, I have
suggested no guests at mealtimes and after seven p.m. at night. I
have also stipulated that no guests are allowed to stay overnight,
even small children. I understand that your staff wish to make
Pilgrim House like a family home, but while I appreciate the sen-
timent, I am sure we are all agreed that there are limits.

I would also like to draw your attention to the doodles on the
latest staff notice. I appreciate Sophi (Sophie?) might be young,
but I still think childish scribbles are unnecessary and take away
from the seriousness of the information she is imparting. Even
lunch menus contribute to the smooth running of the house and
so should be shown respect.

Yours sincerely,
George Griffiths

48. LETTER FROM MARTIN MORRIS TO MO GRIFFITHS

Dear Mo,

I can't stop thinking about the old studio now. Do you remember how it always smelled as if something was burning? You used
to make me go around and check the lights. Once, I switched

them all off and pretended it was too dark to see where you were. I called for you, Mo, just to hear you answer. But then I tripped over the lead and all the photographs from that afternoon's session went flying. You were pleased, I think. You were always too jealous of the other girls. I never looked at them in that way, not then. They were just canvases for where the light should fall. You *were* the light, Mo. It was never the same after you went back to George. I tried, but somehow everything lost its meaning.

At the newsagent's, I used to look at men poking around on the top shelf and I'd want to shoo them away. It was the kiddies I liked best. The way they'd come in with pennies saved from their pocket money and I'd make up selections of sweets for them. "You do it best, Mr. Morris," they'd say if Mahad tried to serve them. I wonder if they knew how many extra I'd put in? For years, I used to look and see if one of them was Nell. Long after she must have gone to high school, but still I'd stare at the young ones. I was the same about you. I knew when you were thirty, and then forty, and then fifty, but I never thought of you like that.

There was a school party in here yesterday. They sang "The Lord Is My Shepherd" in French. I would have preferred English but I clapped hard anyway. One little chap didn't open his mouth, just stood at the back picking his nose. "Didn't your mother ever tell you that was rude?" Helen said when they'd finished, but he shook his head. When we were having our tea, Brenda said we weren't supposed to say things about mothers and fathers in case they didn't have one. It was against the rules apparently. "Ridiculous," George said, and for once everyone agreed with him.

Robyn came in again just after. "Have you seen your granddad?" I asked her.

She looked worried then. "No," she said, "I thought I'd see you first." She was hemming and hawing as if something exciting had happened.

"What is it?" I asked her. "Got ants in your pants?"

She laughed at that. Seems all the expressions we took for normal are quaint now. "I've written a poem about Annabel Armstrong," she said. "I want you to read it. You know how you said about her waist and stuff. I tried to do what you told me and imagined her as a young person."

"Quite," I said.

"But it's a bit naughty." She clutched a corner of the piece of paper until I had to pull it away from her.

"You'll tell me what you think," she said. I nodded.

"And you won't tell granddad? I'm not sure he'd like it."

I read it quickly, trying not to look up at her. It was about Annabel's longing for the parrots to see how clever she was, as well as beautiful, and there were lines and lines about the trees Annabel could see from her window.

"Not bad." I passed it back to her.

"You didn't like it?" She looked like one of the little French singers we'd just had, standing there and biting her bottom lip.

"I think you could have gone further," I said. "Really tried to explore the side of someone no one else knows about."

"Further?" She scanned the poem, and I could see her hands were shaking.

"Shock me," I said. "The best artists are always the ones who take the most risks. Perhaps you could say something about Annabel's lovers?"

She nodded, and folded up the poem once and then again very carefully, corner to corner. I used to wonder whether it was worth it. You leaving me to be with your girls. But I think I know the answer to that now. They put themselves so completely in your hands, don't they?

M

49. LETTER FROM FLORENCE OLIVER TO LIZZIE CORN

Dear Lizzie,

I couldn't believe it when I read your letter and learned it wouldn't be convenient for me to come to stay with you after all. In fact, I swore out loud with disappointment at the breakfast table, and Brenda Lewis heard me. "Everything all right?" she trilled.

"Fine," I said, otherwise she'd be fussing over me all day, but it's not. I can't pretend it is.

Of course, I understand completely that family comes first, and that with Troy more and more around the house, Laurie doesn't feel able to cope with a guest. But I'm only small, Lizzie, and I'd be tucked away in your room so there would be no need for Laurie to clear out the spare room. I'm sad not to see you. I miss you. I love you.

There I've said it. And now you'll call me a silly old fool. Well, you've called me worse over the years.

To tell the truth, I'm a bit down for other reasons. The seduction isn't going all that well. I asked George if he wanted me to give him a quick rub on his stiff shoulder the other night and he threatened to call Brenda, accusing me of molestation. I had to look it up in the dictionary to make sure I'd got it right. We've only got a Scrabble one here so it's not all that helpful unless the word you want starts with a Q or has two letters, but I wasn't molesting anyway. The idea of it!

It's just that Martin suggested I should try and make physical contact because apparently that's very effective. Afterward, he told me that he meant just touch George lightly on the arm but Graham always used to get me to rub around his neck after he'd been on the parade ground. I'd have been on my feet all day keeping the house as clean as he liked it, but Graham just called that women's work. Nice and cushy, he'd say, although he'd be looking around for spots I'd missed even while I was standing there rubbing his pimply neck and worrying about the dinner burning.

So what to do now about George? Martin says I've got to come up with something on my own. He says it's because he's busy with the granddaughter. Robyn, she's called.

Anyway, you have a think. You always were the clever one. And I'll try to get over my disappointment about not seeing you. Let's look for a nice place to go in the summer, shall we? I've got this postcard up in my room from George's daughter in Paris. It's one of the ones I stole but imagine a boat trip on the Seine. Would it be too much for us to try a bit of abroad for ourselves?

Yours aye,
Flo

50. ANSWER PHONE MESSAGE FROM
    CLAUDE BICHOURIE TO ANGELA GRIFFITHS

Angela, unexpectedly I find myself free again this evening. After last night, I have been longing to see you, just to spend more time with my Saxon queen of the dark eyes and the dark temper. So I will be with you at seven. No need to cook, we will go out, or we will think of other ways of taking our pleasure. Prepare for me well. I will like to think of that in my meetings today.

51. ANSWER PHONE MESSAGE FROM
    DOCTOR FLAUBERT TO ANGELA GRIFFITHS

Madame Griffiths, further to your consultation with Dr. Flaubert today, we would like to confirm that your test results are positive. Dr. Flaubert has asked me to pass on his congratulations and would be grateful if you could call us at your earliest convenience to arrange a second appointment to discuss possible courses of action.

52. LETTER FROM BRENDA LEWIS TO NELL BAKER

Dear Nell,

A power-point presentation does sound a treat! I'm sure it will be very nice indeed for the residents to have something so exciting to look forward to.

However, I did have a little concern as to whether "Food—past, present and future" might be a touch too ambitious. It could be that a more practical session would go down better. We have just had a very successful demonstration here on making sugar-icing flowers by Catherine Francis's former cleaning lady, of which the highlight was when the residents were allowed to place iced flowers on a cake Mrs. Cooper had brought with her. We do welcome any chance to empower our ladies and gentlemen.

On another matter, you should know that your father has taken to insisting our young work-experience helper, Sophi, brings him cups of tea in his room with extra biscuits. Not only is this inconveniencing our staff, but he seems to believe for some reason that he is not getting his fair share of the provisions available for all our residents and is therefore determined to increase his portions. As you know, part of our philosophy here at Pilgrim House is to foster a community spirit, and it is such a shame when one of our residents doesn't feel able to take full advantage of all that entails. As you know, we set great store by the friendships our residents form with each other. It may be that if your father continues to be unhappy with the way things are run, then he would be more suited to another establishment, much as we would obviously hate to lose him.

Do let me know what you decide to do for your talk. We are always invigorated by the chance to partake in the outside world.

Yours sincerely,
Brenda Lewis

53. EMAIL FROM NELL BAKER TO ANGIE GRIFFITHS

Of course, I didn't mean to blame you for Mum's death. It's just that it's fine and dandy to talk about doing what's right for you, but not everyone can do that.

I'm not trying to keep us all glued together, and I can't see how you can say I'm smothering you. I never forced you to tell me why you left, or why you suddenly made contact again just after Robyn was born. I asked Mum and she said to leave it because it was up to you, so I did. We were all grown-ups, after all, but you can't blame me for wondering sometimes. And you are still Dad's daughter as much as I am, which is why I'm asking for help with him.

Let's change the subject. You know this talk I'm going to do at Pilgrim House, well, I'm determined to prove Brenda wrong about what the oldies are interested in. OK, I have an ulterior motive in that I'd really like Dad to understand what I do. I thought one way might be to talk about all the food Mum used to cook for us, and then compare it with what families might eat in the future. Maybe it is ambitious, but even so. When I'm that age, I want to be aiming a little higher than being applauded for putting decorations on cakes.

Anyway, I've been trying to remember some of Mum's old recipes. What was that secret ingredient she used to be so proud of in her flapjacks? And don't laugh, but do you know how to make shepherd's pie? I don't expect you're doing anything so mundane anymore, but you were always in the kitchen with her so you must have picked up something. Trouble is I don't seem to have a recipe book. James took all of ours with him when he left, and I seem to have missed out on the domestic gene.

Any idea when you're coming yet? Brenda sent a bit of a threatening letter about Dad needing a new place to stay so I guess I'll have to do some peacekeeping there. She's been hinting that I should encourage Dad to make friends with the other residents. Dad! You have to laugh sometimes.

54. LETTER FROM MARTIN MORRIS TO MO GRIFFITHS

Dear Mo,

Remember I told you about the twins next door? They were out again this afternoon. I was taking a walk around our garden when I heard scuffling on the other side of the wall. I stopped, and the noise stopped. Took a few more steps, and it started again. Stopped, and there was a giggle and then silence. So I coughed. *Herhum, herhum,* came back from their side.

I'd have loved to have hoisted myself up the wall and surprised them, but I didn't want to do myself an injury so I said loudly, "I do wish there were some small boys around who might answer me a few questions in reply for a shilling or two." I had two faces looking down at me straightaway.

"You don't get shillings anymore," said one of them.

"We did them in history," said the other.

"And farthings."

"Stupid, they were bicycles. Not money."

And with that, the one who had mentioned farthings pushed the other off the wall.

"Can you remember life without electricity?" the remaining one said to me. "We have to do a project on it for school. Borrring."

I was still trying not to laugh when the second one popped up again. "You can't ask him," he said. "It has to be all our own work."

"He could be an Original Source," the first one said. "Mr. Winston said we could ask grandparents."

They both looked at me a bit doubtfully.

"We've got no grandparents," the first boy said. "They were all killed by a bomb. All four of them. It was most unfortunate."

"Liar. You know what Mum said about your lying." And both boys disappeared then. I could hear them fighting in the flower bed, and then a cry of "Bayzz, bayzz!" from the house.

"Shit, it's Marta," the first boy popped back up to tell me. "We've got to go now, otherwise she will beat us. She always does. But nice talking to you. Think about the electricity thing, won't you?"

"And our money," the second boy said.

"What money?" I could hear the first one asking as they went back inside.

"He promised us some for talking to him."

I was left shaking my head. I wished I could have spent longer with them. I would have said how we would walk around with our eyes shut to get used to the darkness without electric lights. I thought they might copy that in the yard and I could have some fun watching them.

Just then, a foreign voice came from the other side of the wall. "I am sorry if you were disturbed," it said. "They have been told to leave you alone."

"No, no," I said. It was strange talking to bricks. "They are fine boys."

"In my country, they would be taught manners," the voice said. "But Mummy and Daddy here say no tellings-off, so they are growing like wild men."

I wanted to see what she looked like. I told her again it was all right, and then I went back up to my room. I pulled up a chair and watched for what seemed like hours. At first it was just the boys, playing at what looked like robots. And then, finally, she came out. Tiny, her blond hair scraped back under a baseball cap, and a tight, beaky face. "Get her," the first boy shouted, and the second rushed at her. She ran back inside the house screaming.

"Marta beats us," I remembered, and I laughed all over again. She must have been about twenty, but she was almost smaller than them. I have been trying to work out which bedroom might be hers. If I stand at the very back of the lawn, I can get a good view of their house. There are two small windows at the top, at the same level as mine. I think one of them might be hers. It's comforting to think of her lying there on the other side of the wall to me. Two lost souls together,

M

55. LETTER FROM FLORENCE OLIVER TO LIZZIE CORN

Dear Lizzie,

I forgive you for not having me to stay now because you are a genius. Of course, men can never resist giving advice. Now why didn't I think of that myself? And I have just the thing. George is always going on about his accountancy background so I will ask him about investments. I can ask him what to do with the money Graham left me. He doesn't have to know that it is all secure.

But how worrying for you that Troy has moved in full-time. And although I did laugh when I read about him wearing a sarong at the breakfast table, I can see you are anxious with Amy being so young and curious. I won't ask how you can be so sure he didn't have anything on underneath. I have heard them say such things before about Scotsmen, but Troy's from Birmingham, isn't he?

It's all go here. We had someone come in to talk to us from the gas board about getting old yesterday. Brenda got her tentacles into him when he came to read the meter, and you can imagine how it's impossible to say no to her. He sweated a lot so we all felt sorry for him. Anyway, he didn't say anything, just kept taking things out of this box he'd brought with him and putting them on. First he had some big rubber gloves that he half filled with water and then slipped on his hands. Trouble was they were so tight they made this loud farting noise that we tried not to notice. He glared at us then and rammed two garden sticks down the arm-holes of his coat so the ends stuck out and when he turned around, he poked Annabel in the chest. After she'd calmed down, he smeared these plastic spectacles with cream and put them on and then he just stood there, staring at us. It was a bit frightening so we all looked back until eventually he said this is how the gas company taught their staff what it felt like to be us. Apparently he'd been sent on a weekend course on dealing with old people.

"Very nice," said Brenda. "I think we find it immensely reas-suring to know how our needs are being listened to." No one knew what to say until Annabel Armstrong chipped in to ask if he was going to tell us some jokes. "He's a funny man," she kept say-ing. "Hit him hard so he rolls over." She must have thought he was a clown. Brenda started clapping then, although Keith said after-ward that we should have all said we couldn't clap because our hands were too full of water. If I were Keith and could get out, I don't think I'd stay for our social talks but he does like to stay close to Beth.

Next month, we are getting a talk from George's daughter. Not the one in Paris, that would be a treat, but the one who comes in here all the time. The tired one. Brenda says she is going to talk to us about trend forecasting. Even George isn't exactly sure what that is, although he said it was like a glorified secretary, but after he'd gone Helen said it was obviously to do with fortune-telling. I hope not. Remember we went to that one in a Gypsy caravan in

Brighton who said Graham was looking out for me from the other side. It gave me the shivers for weeks, thinking of him watching me. But then I got to rather like it, leaving out the dishes, eating chocolate for breakfast, and even turning up my skirts at the waistband like a schoolgirl so you could see my knees. All the things I knew Graham would hate. You can't get me now, I thought, but it was still a bit worrying. Just in case.

And now you must excuse me. I have some homework to do if I am going to find the right questions for George.

Yours aye,
Flo

56. LETTER FROM GEORGE GRIFFITHS TO BRENDA LEWIS

Dear Mrs. Lewis,

As I was waiting in the reception this morning, I couldn't help but notice that the pile of envelopes waiting to be taken to the mailbox had first-class stamps on them. Given that we are all being asked to tighten our belts and we are living in a charitable institution, I wondered whether it might be a useful exercise to consider whether some letters were not so urgent and could therefore travel by second-class. We seem to have got into a situation where rush-rush is the order of the day, and although it may seem like a trivial saving, as an ex-accountant, I know only too well the truth of the adage, "take care of the pennies and the pounds will take care of themselves."

I hope you do not mind me bringing this to your attention. My offer to assist you in the office, or at least to undertake an audit of the administration of Pilgrim House, remains open anytime you would wish to take me up on this.

Yours sincerely,
George Griffiths

57. LETTER FROM MARTIN MORRIS TO MO GRIFFITHS

Dear Mo,

Well, I finally got around to reading the second draft of the poem Robyn wrote. It made even me blush. No wonder she was nervous. I did tell her that if she wanted to be a proper writer, then she had to take risks, but maybe *Lady Chatterley's Lover* wasn't the best book to recommend to her for ideas. Or maybe it was. She's seventeen, after all. For all her piercings and bravado, she has been babied by her mother.

I told her that maybe she wouldn't want Nell to find the poem so I'd keep it safe for her. "Did you really like it?" she asked.

"I thought it wonderfully written," I lied. "You should go through the other residents and imagine lives for them like that."

"But is that OK? It feels a bit as if I'm taking something from them." There are times when she's so puppylike you long to kick her. Anyway, I told her it was all about creating a persona.

"It's how all artists create," I told her. "We do the same in photography. You start with the basics, but it's the artist who makes it interesting." And then of course she wanted to see some of my photographs.

"Another time," I said. "I'm tired now." But she asked who she should write about next. I said Catherine Francis might be good, and when she looked doubtful, I told her how Catherine's great sadness was how she had always loved women but had to keep it a secret until now.

I had a moment of wondering whether I had gone too far when young Robyn put her hand over her mouth, but in these situations all you can do is to make the story bigger. "That's why we're all so pleased she has become so friendly with Helen Elliott," I continued. I could see which way Robyn's mind was working.

"Mum says Granddad's not pleased," she said, clutching tighter at her mouth.

"Exactly," I said. "He's always had a soft spot for Catherine, hasn't he?"

"Granddad has?"

I looked at Robyn closer. Trouble with all that makeup is that you can't always see whether she is worried or about to burst out laughing. "You have to explore the whole world if you want to be a writer," I said. "And that means being interested in everything to do with people, not just what you want to see. No use hiding in nature."

And she left. She darts in and out of here as if she's scared she's going to be spotted. Worried about her grandfather, I should imagine, because I told her that he'd hinted she upset him.

She looked crestfallen, so I'd said that sometimes when you get old, you don't see things properly and the kindest thing was to let people be. I told her I'd put in a good word for her and her granddaddy.

"I don't understand it myself," I said. "But perhaps we should just leave him alone for the minute."

Or perhaps she was anxious about coming across Catherine and Helen in a clinch.

I put her poem in one of the new folders I'd borrowed from George's room. But not before I looked at it again. I couldn't meet Annabel Armstrong's eyes at supper, I can tell you. Mrs. Oliver had to nudge me to pass the salt, and George gave me one of his looks. Luckily Steve had joined us, so he kept us all amused talking about something called "Ebay." It seems he is buying pots, cleaning them, and selling them for double in the antiques shops around town.

"But is that morally sound?" George asked.

"Who cares?" Steve said, although it was only afterward when George had gone that he told us that all the money he makes goes toward a youth club he runs. You should have seen Florence's face. It was pure love. I filed it away too, that look.

M

58. NOTE FROM CLAUDE BICHOURIE TO
ANGELA GRIFFITHS

My little English Angela, it bores me when we argue. Our time together should be spent on love and joy. I have asked my bank to increase your allowance because, of course, you must have more clothes. But be careful how you ask me next time. There are ways these things could be prettier done.

59. NOTE FROM STEVE JENKINS TO GEORGE GRIFFITHS

George,
    Keith Crosbie, Martin Morris, and myself thought we might put together a darts team at the local Wednesday nights. Care to join us? We thought we'd call ourselves The Pilgrims, have T-shirts made and the like. Just a bit of fun.

Steve

60. NOTE FROM GEORGE GRIFFITHS TO
STEVE JENKINS (WRITTEN ON NOTE 59)

DEAR George,
    Keith Crosbie (WHO IS NOT A RESIDENT), Martin Morris and ~~myself~~ I thought we might put together a darts team ~~at~~ FOR the FALCON ARMS ~~local~~ ON Wednesday nights (TIME?). WOULD YOU LIKE ~~Care~~ to join us? We thought we'd call ~~ourselves~~ OUR TEAM The Pilgrims (DISRESPECTFUL?), have T-shirts made and the like (THE LIKE? BE SPECIFIC). IT IS just a bit of fun (THE FUN ELEMENT IS ENTIRELY SUBJECTIVE).
    WITH BEST WISHES/YOURS SINCERELY/OR EVEN FROM

Steve

Dear Steve,

Thank you for your invitation but I find myself busy on Wednesday evenings. I wish you well in your endeavor, though.

With best wishes,
George

61. EMAIL FROM NELL BAKER TO ANGIE GRIFFITHS

YOU'RE WHAT?!!! My kid sister pregnant! I'm guessing you haven't told Dad yet. He's going to go ballistic. Still, congratulations. It's not the married Monsieur Frog, is it? Does he know? You'll have to speak to Dad when he's here. Don't you dare do it by one of your postcards and leave me to pick up the pieces. Hey, you realize this will mean you'll be the bad girl now and he can stop going on about my divorce. Maybe he'll even let Robyn off the hook. His latest escapade is to have upset one of the care workers. Brenda said "enough is enough" and I had to have a word with him. I was nearly sick with nerves on the way there, but he was surprisingly cooperative. I'd forgotten about his sudden shifts. It's as if he needs to get it out of his system and then he's fine, although I still can't help but think he's got something up his sleeve. Oh, a baby, Angie. I can't believe it. You of all people. Tell me more.

62. ANSWER PHONE MESSAGE FROM
ANTOINE DUPERT TO ANGELA GRIFFITHS

If you don't want to talk to me, at least look at the photographs we created together. You can't tell me they don't show the connection between us. We made the earth move then, and after. We made every cliché true. If I don't hear from you, I will get my staff to call you. No one as beautiful as you can make themselves as invisible as you seem to have done.

63. ANSWER PHONE MESSAGE FROM THE OFFICE OF DR. FLAUBERT TO ANGELA GRIFFITHS

Madame Griffiths, this is Dr. Flaubert's office again. Dr. Flaubert would like to remind you of the urgency of scheduling your second appointment as soon as possible. Please could you call. Thank you.

64. LETTER FROM GEORGE GRIFFITHS TO BRENDA LEWIS

Dear Mrs. Lewis,

I have just been to my room to find my copy of *Accountancy Age* is missing, as well as several items of stationery. Given that I am the only resident in Pilgrim House with professional qualifications and the magazine can therefore be of no interest to others, I am forced to come to the conclusion that these thefts are of a personal nature, designed purely to annoy. I would be grateful if you could reconsider your position about locks on residents' doors as I am sure my daughter could arrange this with no inconvenience to yourself.

On that other matter, and further to a conversation with my daughter, I have today apologized to Steve for his misunderstanding of my well-meaning attempt to correct his written English. I hope that will be the end to it. For Nell's sake, I will endeavor to partake in the fruits of social contact with my fellow residents.

Yours sincerely,
George Griffiths

65. LETTER FROM MARTIN MORRIS TO MO GRIFFITHS

Dear Mo,

Truth is I didn't expect to find it so tiring being with other people. Maybe it's because I'm out of practice, but it seems you say one thing to them only to have them come back with another and then you've got to think of something else altogether to say. It's like a game of Ping-Pong.

At least when I was behind the camera I had something to fiddle with. Same with the shop. People would come in and I'd only have to make a comment about the weather, or the state of the world, and they'd be out the door again. If they tried to stay a bit longer, I could pretend something was wrong with the till and I needed to fix it. Mahad and I often spent hours together in silence. It comforted me, and I think him.

I see it with young Marta next door. The boys say she is bolshy. "Where did you get that word from?" I asked them, and they said it's what their mother calls her. It seems her nickname in the family is "Doom and Gloom." I look at her sometimes, standing among the rosebushes at the bottom of the garden, and I know she's not sulking, she's just being. But of course, the boys find her and think she's being bolshy. They threw a stone at her the other day. I told them later that if I caught them doing anything like that ever again, I'd arrange for Steve to whip them. I know they worship Steve because one day when I was watching, I saw him take his top off so they could see his tattoos. They both nearly fell off the wall with excitement.

You were like Marta and me too, happy to enjoy your own company. I see it in your Nell too. I've been trying to make friends with her but she turns herself into a blank wall. Not like Robyn, who is all open doors in her enthusiasm. Strange, because she's the one who looks like she'd be the least friendly. Funny how easy it is to get the wrong impression. Did I tell you what her latest thing is?

She's been on the Internet and found this site that tells her how to live without electricity and buying anything. She even came in the other day with all these plans and drawings she'd made for growing a house out of a tree. You pull the branches down and after about fifty years of watching it grow, you've got walls.

"That'll be ready for when you're my age," I said, and she laughed. She said that she and her dad always used to talk about things like that.

"You could send it to him," I said.

But she just shook her head. "Too much trouble," she said. "I just like thinking about living in a tree."

"People not nature," I reminded her. "When are you going to do another story?"

She's started to ask why I didn't want her talking about her poetry to George. She's too softhearted, I reckon, but I need to build up the relationship between her and me first. What we need is something we can do together, something George has no idea about but that will let me get to her mum too. I reckon the best route to Nell is through her daughter. Mums and daughters, eh? You should know, love.

And now I have to go to make it up to Florence Oliver. I was a bit short with her earlier on account of her going on and on about some pen pal's family, and now I'm feeling remorseful. She just needs to be a bit more pushy with George if she's going to have an impact on him. We need a bit of luck. Don't fancy waving your magic dust our way, do you, love?

M

66. POSTCARD FROM FLORENCE OLIVER TO LIZZIE CORN

Dear Lizzie,

I thought you might like this photograph of Princess Di's grave for your Royal collection. I hope you don't already have it. Just to let you know your "Plan" has worked. I'll say no more now, but wish me luck.

Flo

67. EMAIL FROM NELL BAKER TO ANGIE GRIFFITHS

Nope, of course I won't tell Dad about the baby. What do you think I am, stupid? But what do you mean you haven't decided what to do? Surely you're going to have it. Can I call you?

68. ANSWER PHONE MESSAGE FROM
ANTOINE DUPERT'S STUDIO TO ANGELA GRIFFITHS

Madame Griffiths, this is Antoine's studio. Antoine has asked me to tell you that the photographs from your session are waiting for collection. Would you like us to send them to you? In which case, I would be grateful if you could call us with your address, which seems to be missing from our records.

69. NOTE FROM ROBYN BAKER TO MARTIN MORRIS
(LEFT AT PILGRIM HOUSE)

Dear Martin,

I came to see you today, but Steve said you were in your room and I only had a few minutes in between lessons. Anyway, I wanted you to be the first to know, because guess what! I had a letter from *Open* magazine saying they want to publish one of my poems. It's one about a skylark. I got the idea from those paintings you told me about.

I know it's nature and you don't like that, but they said they wanted to see more too. Mum's going to be well pleased. I've put a copy in the envelope if you feel like reading it. I asked Steve to give this to you and I also made him promise not to tell Granddad as you said. When do you think I can? I'd love him to know I can do something good. I'll take out my piercing if you think that would help. Do you?

Rob

70. ANSWER PHONE MESSAGE FROM
GEORGE GRIFFITHS TO ANGIE GRIFFITHS

Hello Angie, or should I say Angie's machine. We're developing quite a relationship here, the machine and I. It's two thirty on Friday, and I fear I ring with some distressing news.

I have found the culprit for the petty thieving I have been enduring and it has come as a shock to me, as it will to you, that it is a family member. None other than Robyn. I looked out of the window of the sitting room earlier and saw her leaving Pilgrim House. However, when I went down to see whether she had left me a message, there was nothing and apparently she had not asked for me. Obviously I went straight to my room to carry out a thorough check and noted that two of the books on my windowsill had been knocked over. In addition, the book you gave me last Christmas, *The Dummy's Guide to Investment,* is missing. I have always presumed that the book was your idea of a joke, but kept it for sentimental reasons.

Obviously this book can be of no interest to her, so her hooliganism can only be a cry for help. I want Robyn to know that I know, and thus give her the chance to confess. I have always prided myself on being a fair-minded person, and am willing to let bygones be bygones.

It is quiet here today. Two of our residents, Catherine Francis and Helen Elliott, have taken to going out shopping together. I hope this will not be the start of cliques forming. I remember from work that female friendships could often end in tears as women have a natural tendency to become unstable and fall out with each other. However, it seems that the other residents have been asking for me to spend more time with them. Nell told me this, and to be honest it has come at just the right time. I will start to plan and form friendships in an orderly manner.

In fact, I have been thinking for some time that a Residents Committee could be just what is needed here, particularly as there have been many mishaps recently on the administration front. I have often found that firm structures and rules are the best way to maintain the peace we all so much deserve.

Your mother would often let a whole afternoon go by because she had become engrossed with a novel or a book of poems. When I retired, we established a rota of set mealtimes, fixed domestic duties, and leisure time. You, of course, were in France by then, but I think even your mother would admit that things in the house ran more smoothly when we followed my patterns. Sometimes she would be too tired to read in the evening and consequently, less plagued by the worries that could so often beset her.

Anyway, I will keep you informed of events.

Your father

71. LETTER FROM MARTIN MORRIS TO MO GRIFFITHS

Dear Mo,

When I was living on my own, I used to have your photograph out all the time. Now I can only put it up sometimes but I like to look at it when I write to you. Your hands are so tightly fisted by your sides that you look as if you want to punch me. Perhaps you did. "Take my photo," you said that day in the studio. "But you'll not get me to take my clothes off."

I wasn't used to a challenge like that. Most women who came to the studio were desperate to see themselves through someone else's eyes, even mine, and if they had to strip off, then so much the better. But you both wanted it and were scared of it. Were you frightened you might never be able to stop? I put my finger out then, do you remember, and I just touched your cheekbone. It was as if I was wiping away a tear, but you weren't crying, Mo. Not then anyw— oh blow, there's someone at the door.

*

I'm back again. You'll never guess who that was. George. He's never come to my room before. I only just had time to slip your photograph back in the box before he walked in. He stood there for a moment. My heart was thumping in case he'd seen you, but he didn't. He must have seen the other pictures I'd piled on top of you, though.

"Not a thing you forget," he said, standing there as cool as a cucumber. "The sight of a naked woman."

"No," I said, because I didn't know what else to say. We carried on saying nothing like that until he asked if I wanted to go for a walk with him. "With you?" I asked. I thought for a minute he knew something, and this was going to be our big confrontation. At last. Remember that letter I put through your letterbox once, Mo? For the week after, I'd jump every time someone came to the door. I couldn't believe you wouldn't come to me, but I feared it might be him too. Fear and longing. The same feelings I think you had in the studio.

"Yes," he replied, slowly now, as if I wasn't quite getting the message. Which of course I wasn't. "A walk, with me."

"I suppose so," I said. "But give me a bit of time to get ready first."

"I'll be downstairs in half an hour," he said, and then he left without another word. Not even good-bye.

I've got five minutes left before I should go. I just want to finish this letter and then I need to think. The mountain has come to me and I have to play this one right. It's like when Frank Bradley came to the studio that day and told me to come in with him on the magazine operation or stop altogether. I didn't hold my nerve then, but I will now. Wish me luck.

M

72. LETTER FROM NELL BAKER TO MARTIN MORRIS

Dear Mr. Morris,

Robyn has told me how much you helped her with her poem. We are very proud of her recent success, but I had no idea she has been pestering you for help. She has assured me that you have encouraged her visits but please let me know if she is being an inconvenience.

With best wishes, and thanks again,
Nell

73. EMAIL FROM NELL BAKER TO ANGIE GRIFFITHS

God forbid, poor Robyn should actually be allowed to have something good happen to her for the first time in years. I can't believe Dad's been saying she stole from him. As if she would. What on earth would he have that she might want? His athlete's foot cream? After your last email, I asked her straight out and it turns out she was visiting another resident at Pilgrim House who's been helping her with poetry. She'd wanted to thank him.

Anyway, it proves Brenda Lewis was right with her theory that nothing was ever taken from Dad in the first place. He must have been imagining things. Robyn doesn't even want him to know about her poem being published now, and I'm inclined to agree. We are pretty practiced at keeping family secrets, after all. She says he's made it clear he doesn't want to see her too. That's why she's been talking to Martin.

Strange about this Martin Morris, though. Do you think I should be worried he's taking such an interest? I've written to him just to let him know I know about him and Robyn. Best to have it out in the open.

I've just been up to her room and she's ripped Dad's schedule off the wall. Instead she's put up a photograph of a baby fox blinking out from its hole. I guess that's what she feels like. I took the torn up bits of the schedule, though. I didn't want to see them just thrown away.

Where are you by the way? Are you ever at home? You can't be out having fun anymore at least. Not now you're pregnant!

74. LETTER FROM MARTIN MORRIS TO NELL BAKER

Dear Nell,

It has been my pleasure to spend time with Robyn so please don't apologize. She must make you very proud. I have been interested in poetry for a long time, and it is especially heartening to find a young person nowadays who appreciates my old favorites and doesn't find them—and me—too boring. She mentioned that you often quoted from some of the poems we have been looking at. She even thought you might have told her my own particular favorite line, "Love lies beyond the tomb, the earth, which fades like dew! I love the fond, the faithful and the true." If you ever had time to join me for a cup of tea and a talk about poetry, it would make me very happy, but I understand that family visits come first, and, of course, your father may not want to share the pleasure of your company.

Yours,
Martin

75. LETTER FROM MARTIN MORRIS TO MO GRIFFITHS

Dear Mo,

I've just written to Nell. It was so strange. I wanted to ask if she remembered coming to my studio when she was a little girl. She must have only been about three or four. Remember how you made me take all the pictures down from everywhere and put them in a cupboard. It took hours. You brushed her hair and sat her on the stool, but you wouldn't let me take her photograph. I loved to see you brush her hair, the comfort you gave her, the love.

Many years later, I watched you both walking down the street. She was a teenager by then, too old to touch really, but I saw you just lift your hand and touch her hair at the back. I don't think she even noticed, or if you wanted her to. You held your fingers a few inches from her head and then, I'll never forget this, you put your hand up to your face and shut your eyes. You were inhaling your daughter.

It doesn't look as if anyone has brushed Nell's hair or loved her like that for years. But don't you fear, if I couldn't save you, I'll save her.

M

76. EMAIL FROM NELL BAKER TO ANGIE GRIFFITHS

Me again. Just to say how wrong can you be? I got a letter from that old man at Pilgrim House. You know, the one Robyn had been talking about poetry with, and he's only invited me to have tea with him.

His letter made me shiver because he quoted that line Mum always used to go on about, you know, the one about loving going on after you've died. Hah, I wish James had listened to that being-true-and-faithful bit.

Anyway, this Martin made me cry, saying I should be proud of Robyn.

I can't remember the last time anyone told me that. And to think I told Dad to make friends with him. What have I let this Martin in for?

I think I'm going to accept his invitation to tea. Just him and me, away from Pilgrim House. Dad doesn't need to know. You could be right about Robyn looking for a father figure, but she knows she can see James whenever she wants. It's her decision, and neither of us have put any pressure on her either way.

And about the other thing, I'm glad you've decided to have the baby. You're not alone and you can always come here. Anytime. We can make arrangements when you're over. It's not too late for us to be a family, surely. Robyn would love it. In his defense, Dad asked her to go to tea the other day but I said she didn't have to if she didn't want to, so she said no. I told her I was proud of her. Perhaps I should start saying it a bit more often.

77. LETTER FROM FLORENCE OLIVER TO LIZZIE CORN

Dear Lizzie,

Well, you can release your breath and uncross your fingers. George and I had our meeting and that's all it was. A business meeting. He'd even drawn up an agenda. Point number one was "Explain that investments can go up as well as down." It felt like the time I had to go in and see the bank manager after Graham died and he asked me if I knew how a credit card worked. Admittedly Graham never liked me to shop, but who did the manager think had been balancing the books for years? Rather well too it seems, according to this manager. "Do you know how much money your husband has left you?" he asked, and I got a little satisfaction from seeing his face when I told him the exact amount down to the last penny.

Remember that investment club we started on the army base

when the men were away on the German tour? We made a fair packet, and it taught me a lot.

Anyway, I was a good girl and played dumb with George. I couldn't quite manage the "you're so clever" line, but I sat still while he went through points two to ten, pretended I'd never heard of an IRA or compound interest. Trouble is, for no reason at all, I got this picture of George pleasing himself on a bed of pound notes, and that was it. I thought I was going to burst with giggles. Daft of me. He looked a bit cross and put away his file. Did I tell you about his file? He's got this black clipboard, with a pencil taped to a piece of string. He does make me think of Graham. He was always tying ballpoints to the phone or to the calendar in the kitchen because he thought I would hide them to spite him. Well, I did, but it's in the same way I take things from George's room. Some men need to worry about the small things, otherwise who knows what they'll get it into their heads to start accusing you of.

So to cut a long story short, George has left me to have a think. He's written out some notes and I'm to come back to him. He's got it a bit wrong because I'd be leaving myself open on the futures front with the plan he's given me, so I'll have to come up with a way of not letting on about that, but at least we managed to spend some time together without me losing my temper at him too much and there's another meeting planned. Martin will be pleased about that.

The only time he seemed human was when he mentioned Robyn toward the end. I said I was sure I'd seen her around. He went a bit blustery then and said he had to go. Teenagers are always awkward.

And now I'm off to read the financial pages again. Slowly slowly catches tiger, or is it lamb? I can't remember.

Yours aye,

Flo

78. LETTER FROM MARTIN MORRIS TO MO GRIFFITHS

Dear Mo,

Silly old fool that I am, I was enjoying keeping you waiting until I told you what went on with George. But then I thought hang on a minute, who am I kidding? If I don't speak to you, then you're not exactly going to come chasing after me.

And now it's your husband knocking on my door.

I thought he was joking when he said we could go for a walk because it was raining brass monkeys out there, but it turned out he meant it. He was actually tapping his fingers on the reception desk by the time I got down, his coat all buttoned up and his scarf neatly wrapped around his neck. He gave my getup a bit of a look. I've taken to wearing tracksuits because elasticized waists are a godsend now my fingers aren't too clever, but I could tell he thought it was letting the side down.

We set off around the yard. I could see Brenda Lewis looking out at us from her window so I started talking lively-like because I thought that on the whole it might do me good if it came out I was friendly with George. The others would be relieved I was taking him off their backs. Keith Crosbie in particular is always threatening to deck him, although when Keith's with Beth and they're BethandKeith, it's all smiles and let's keep everything lovely for Beth, so I don't think George realizes.

"So," I started, but then I couldn't think of anything to say and I just nodded a few times. He looked at me a bit strangely though, so I had to go on. I've learned to talk about children and families with the other residents, but I didn't want to go there. Not with him. "I didn't always want to take photographs of women, you know," I lied. I was going to say I wanted to be an accountant like him, or something that would make him feel easy, but then the words kept tumbling out. It was nerves, of course. There I was walking around the lawn with your husband, and all I knew was that I shouldn't mention you.

"I can understand that," he said. "It must have been a strange profession."

That got to me, but I managed to keep my temper. "No," I repeated, "I wanted to be a dancer."

Well, that was a shock. Even to me. I could see him trying not to laugh and I had some sympathy. A dancer, me? I was thinking of you, Mo, and how much I would have loved to dance with you. "Yes, a ballet dancer," I pushed on. "You know when they spring up so they're frozen in midair for a moment, and then they land firmly back on two feet as if they're discovering their strength all over again. It's like a miracle. You wouldn't believe the muscle power involved. Every bit of your body joining in for that one moment. I'd have liked to have learned how to use my body properly."

The funny thing was that the more I went on, the more I really did want to have been a dancer. George was shaking his head, though.

"Have you ever really looked at dancers?" I asked. I was determined to make my point now. "Well, they even hold their heads, open their eyes, their mouths differently from the rest of us."

He looked down at the ground and I could see he didn't want me to see he was smiling. I decided to press home the advantage by taking umbrage.

"It's not funny," I said.

"No, I'm sorry." But he got out his handkerchief and snorted into it so I could tell he wasn't convinced.

"So what did you want to be?" I asked him.

He stared at me. Stopped laughing then. "An accountant," he said.

"What, when you were four?"

He nodded. I couldn't believe it. Imagine one of those little kids next door wanting to sort out figures rather than be a cowboy or the king or a chimney sweep. Did I ever tell you about the chimney sweep who used to come to my home? I used to follow him around, placing my feet on the black footsteps he left behind. That was a bit like dancing, I suppose.

"It was what my father did," George said. "He always wanted me to take over his firm."

Well, my father was a steelworker but I never wanted to follow him to the works. Anything but. I wasn't going to tell George that, though. He'd only have looked down his nose at me because I wasn't from a professional family. He was, after all, the only professional in Pilgrim House, as he must have told us several hundred times.

"Right," I said instead. I wanted to keep George on my side and I guessed the whole dancer thing wasn't exactly working in my favor. "I suppose it must have been quite exciting sometimes."

But then he surprised me. "Not really," he said. "A train driver. I wanted to be that once."

I tried to look interested but not even his dreams were original. Remember you telling me you wanted to be the fairy at the top of the Christmas tree? And how you once spent all holiday crying because your father wouldn't put you up there. I would have made a tree big enough for you to stand on if you'd have spent even one Christmas with me. You know that. I felt like breaking down your window one Christmas when I saw you'd put up one of those artificial trees. I knew that wouldn't have been your choice.

Anyway, we're going to do the walk again tomorrow and he's going to explain exactly how double-column accounting works. The things I do for you, Mo.

M

79. EMAIL FROM NELL BAKER TO ANGIE GRIFFITHS

I don't care if Dad is upset. If Robyn doesn't want to visit him, that's his fault. He has to learn. And we do too, Angie. He can't have it his own way the whole time.

And what do you mean he wanted to be a ballet dancer? You do talk rot. You can't have been listening to him properly. Either that, or you need a new machine. It's probably worn out from all the complaints he seems to be making to you.

80. LETTER FROM FLORENCE OLIVER TO LIZZIE CORN

Dear Lizzie,

Fancy you keeping those notes from our investment club. I'd forgotten how serious we took ourselves. Still, it was always about more than the money, wasn't it? I used to love thinking about those meetings after the boys came back from Germany and we couldn't get together anymore. Of course, you had Laurie to keep you busy by then, but it was still special for all of us.

I wonder what's happened to the other two members, Karen Enders and Miriam Jones. I lost touch with most of the wives because Graham thought it unnatural for women to spend time with other women. It was all right with you, of course, because of Frank.

The Beechwood Investment Committee. We were right posh, weren't we?

Anyway, this will be very helpful. I have made a list of all the questions we asked ourselves at the beginning to go through with George. I've noticed that lists and bullet points are the sort of thing he likes, and I must admit I find there's something comforting about the sense of order they give too. Don't laugh, but I even went out and got myself a file of my own to keep notes of our meetings in.

So what else have you got squirreled away there? I don't suppose you have any of the photographs they took of us that time we won the bottle of champagne at the Palace Ballrooms, have you? We had to plead with the photographer not to send our picture into the local paper because someone might have told Graham and Frank. It's just that Martin's been talking about taking my picture again, and I thought if you still had those shots I might show them to him. That's how I like to think of myself, almost pretty. There was some trick that photographer must have done with light, I reckon. And that was even before we broke into the bubbly.

Now, I have never heard of these war games Brian has taken up, but are they something like the tin soldiers we had in our day? In which case I'm sure there is nothing for you to fret about. Graham used to keep his in an old biscuit tin at the bottom of the wardrobe. He would get them out sometimes when he couldn't sleep, set up wars on the kitchen table and then wake me up to play the enemy. On second thought, maybe you should worry a little. Although, I have heard these old toys are very valuable nowadays. There was someone going on about it on the *Antiques Roadshow* just last week. I do like it when you can watch their faces to work out whether they are pleased with how much they're offered. They never are, have you noticed that? Even when they suddenly get the chance of lots of money, you can see they are suddenly thinking, is that all? It's as if getting a little bit of something opens up this huge hole instead of filling it.

It is a pity Troy won't let you have a television in the house anymore. There's another good show about models too. The camera keeps catching the girls when they look at each other. I want to be you, they're saying, I want your hair, or your smile, or your body. I asked Sophi the other day if she'd like to be a model. "Oh no," she said. "I want a career." She's going to be a psychologist. I found myself looking at her then, with a gust of hunger. I want to be you, I was thinking.

Of course, George doesn't approve of the model program. Brenda says we're to sort out what we watch between us and he's always after changing the channel to something mind-improving, but we're still better off than you. Could you not even get a small one for your room? I can see that family time is important, but Troy's not even family, is he? And you must miss your Royal programs.

Still, I am glad we have agreed on Bournemouth for summer and that Laurie thinks it suitable. It will be something to look forward to. If we're spared, of course.

Yours aye,
Flo

81. NOTE FROM CLAUDE BICHOURIE TO ANGELA GRIFFITHS

Angela,

Here is your air ticket to Monaco. I will meet you at the hotel, but cars have been arranged for you either side. Reserve your strength for me. I have missed you.

Until then,
Claude

82. ANSWER PHONE MESSAGE FROM ANTOINE DUPERT TO ANGELA GRIFFITHS

I just thought the flowers might make you smile. I did not mean to offend, but when I saw you had returned the envelope with the photographs in without even opening them, it was like a dagger to my heart. They are waiting for you here because I am sure you will want to see them one day. I know what happened in the studio that day and it was beyond knowing. The photographs are proof of that.

83. EMAIL FROM NELL BAKER TO ANGIE GRIFFITHS

What do you mean you can't get over here for another month? Hell, Angie. But I suppose if you're being sick everywhere, then there's nothing you can do. Are you sure you're OK with a French doctor? Don't take any medicine you can't understand. I have heard they make you put pills up very unsavory places. Can't imagine doing that when I was pregnant.

Anyway, I had tea at last with the mysterious Martin Morris, and he's OK. He used to be a photographer but obviously something went wrong because he ended up running a newsagent shop instead. It felt a bit rude to ask him too much but he obviously knows all about art and books. Anyway, he's agreed to help coach Robyn, which could be just what she needs. I can't believe my luck. He took some persuading because he didn't want to upset Dad. I ask you. As if Dad would notice anything apart from not getting his dinner at exactly the right time. But to make Martin feel better, I said I'd send a taxi to pick him up and he could meet Robyn here at the house so Dad wouldn't know. They're going to meet weekly at first and we'll see how it goes.

For some reason he makes me think of Mum, probably because they're interested in the same books. He picked up her copy of *The Mayor of Casterbridge*. Asked if he could borrow it. I said yes, although it's always the same with books. The minute someone wants to borrow one, you suddenly want to read it again. Mum loved that one too, didn't she?

I made him some butterfly cakes. I had to scrape the top off where they were a little burned, but he seemed to appreciate them. I was thinking about how Mum used to scoop out a circle at the top and cut it into wings, but I couldn't quite get it like that. Robyn said they were more like beetle cakes, and I told them both how I cried once because I thought the cakes were full of butterflies and Dad sent me to bed because I was spoiling teatime. I think it might have been you who told me about the butterflies now but it was probably just meant to be a joke. I was too scared of everything.

Anyway, Robyn and Martin laughed. He asked a lot about you. She's the beautiful one, I said. I think I wanted Robyn to say, no she isn't, Mum, you are, but she just nodded. It was Martin who said I was beautiful. Very quietly, when Robyn was out of the kitchen. He's an old man, of course, so there's no funny business there but it still made me feel happy.

Anyway, let me know when you can come and you'll let Dad know about the baby, won't you?

84. LETTER FROM MARTIN MORRIS TO MO GRIFFITHS

Dear Mo,

Did you never think of teaching your daughter how to cook? When I think of the treats you once made for us on my little studio gas cooker, my mouth still waters. I'm not sure what it was that Nell made for me yesterday but it tasted like ashes. Robyn couldn't eat it either. I caught her eye after I took a bite and she gestured to something just behind her. It was the wastebasket! So I passed the cake to Robyn without Nell seeing and that was fine.

Anyway, apart from the attempted poisoning, the visit went off so well that she's only invited me around there once a week to spend some time with Robyn.

"I'm not very good at arty things," Nell said. "It was always Robyn's father's specialty."

"Do you see him, Robyn?" I asked. I wanted to include her in the conversation too, so it wouldn't feel I'd been foisted on her by Nell.

She started fiddling with her hair. That's something she does,

Mo, when she's not sure what to say. It's how I'd take her photograph, looking slightly to the side and one hand half covering her face.

"I'd like to," she said then. I could hear Nell's surprised gasp behind me, but I didn't turn around. "But later, when I'm older," Robyn said quickly then.

I wondered after, when I got home, whether she'd heard Nell's gasp too. Probably wanted to protect her mother. I haven't got to grips yet with what caused that marriage breakup, but I'll find out from George. It's all things to store away, Mo. Haven't I always said that nothing is ever wasted!

M

85. ANSWER PHONE MESSAGE FROM
GEORGE GRIFFITHS TO ANGIE GRIFFITHS

Hello Angie,

This is your father. Thank you for your postcard of Rudolf Nureyev. I think you are a little mistaken because it wasn't me that wanted to be a ballet dancer, and I am shocked you should think so. It was another man here and I told you only because it was a disturbing conversation.

This is something I feel it is important to clear up. Wishful thinking is all well and good, but far better to appreciate what life gives you. I have always been very proud to have been an accountant.

Other than this we are all fine. I stubbed my big toe on a textbook young Sophi had left out for Mrs. Oliver, but Nell took me to the doctor. How she manages to take so much time off work I have no idea, but of course her job is not as pressurized as yours.

I wrote to Brenda about the book and the importance all residents must take with their possessions. It could have been much worse.

Your father

86. NOTE FROM MARTIN MORRIS TO ROBYN BAKER

Dear Robyn,

Your poem about Susan Reed shows just how well you are learning to use your imagination. All writers go through the concern you described about using real people for inspiration, but it can be good to feel guilty because you need to break through the resistance and shock yourself. People rarely recognize themselves in writing, and besides, you must trust me not to let your stories fall into the wrong hands. It may be that you want to try to write a group scene soon, perhaps using Pilgrim House as a setting. Just a thought.

It seems to me that this would be much better for your development than more nature poems. Plenty of time for those later.

Martin

87. LETTER FROM DR. CROFT TO BRENDA LEWIS

Dear Ms. Lewis,

Thank you for your letter dated 27 April. I am pleased that my patient, Martin Morris, has settled in so well at Pilgrim House. Certainly, I would not have expected him to be called an "asset" to the social life of any community, and I think you are being modest at not taking the credit for yourself. Let us hope that this will be the change his health so badly needs.

I can understand that you are perturbed that he will not allow anyone in to clean his room. It may be that for the moment, given what you say about his improved personal hygiene, that we would be better to humor him in this matter and trust that his good progress continues. It may just be that he needs time to acclimatize to the lack of privacy.

In the meantime, please keep me informed of any events you think I should know about. I was interested he had been inquiring about Mahad Jefferies, but I am afraid he is correct in that the telephone number for Mr. Jefferies is now registering as unattainable and we have no forwarding address for him. Furthermore, the shop has been turned into an interior decorating consultancy, but I will leave it to your discretion whether you let Mr. Morris know this or not.

Yours sincerely,
Michael Croft

88. LETTER FROM FLORENCE OLIVER TO LIZZIE CORN

Dear Lizzie,

I'm very sorry, I'm sure, if I've had things of my own to talk about recently, and that I forgot to ask about Laurie's concerns about early menopause and Brian's schoolwork, but if I'm being honest, sometimes all you do is whine about your family. How can I be expected to remember and care for every petty thing that happens to people who, if you remember, didn't want me to stay with them because they'd rather have a room free in which to play table football?

I may be silly sometimes, Lizzie, but I am never stupid.

This time I am too hurt to grovel, but I am enclosing a postcard of Marie Antoinette. I know she is French, but she is still Royal. Sorry it is secondhand but George's daughter has lovely handwriting, doesn't she? Very flowery.

Yours aye,
Florence

89. LETTER FROM MARTIN MORRIS TO MO GRIFFITHS

Dear Mo,

There are these two girls who come here every Tuesday to do the ladies' hair. They're called Chrissie and Tina and they set up shop in one of the bathrooms. You should see how serious they take it, like us when you used to come to the studio sometimes and I would set the table for tea beforehand so it would feel like we were living in a proper home.

Anyway, they let me sit on a chair outside in the corridor and watch. They call it Martin's chair now, and they're always joking that if I sit there long enough, they'll do my hair. But then they always say I'm lovely, like their best granddad.

I like to be among the women, and I'm safe from George. He buzzes around me now, but he won't come near "women's morning." Mrs. Oliver says it's because he's worried he'll catch something. I felt sorry for her this morning, and not just because the lipstick she's taken to wearing was smudged so she looked clown-like. She's normally one of these cheery sorts, never letting herself get down, but she seems to have lost her bounce. I wondered if George is being a bit harsh on her. He told me she was "not quite the thing," yesterday. It made my stomach tighten when I thought of you. I hope you didn't always have to be "quite" and never too much, Mo, because God knows you could be too much sometimes. I loved it.

But here I am getting carried away and losing the point of what I was telling you. "I was wondering if you ever thought of growing your hair," I asked Mrs. Oliver. "It would look smashing pinned up." She tut-tutted in that way she always does, but I noticed her hand going up to her hair after like a small furtive mouse. She's hardly a beauty, probably never has been, but I of all people should know that doesn't mean anything. That's why it's important to tell women they're beautiful. It's such a little thing, and you get this glow off them that feels like a candle you've lit yourself. Especially when they're not beautiful. The funny thing is that there are plenty of good-looking women you'd never look at twice because they don't believe it themselves. And plenty more you did more than look at because they thought themselves gorgeous. Think about your friend, Trisha. She wasn't exactly a conventional beauty, was she? And yet she had something.

Don't you be getting jealous again. I need to bolster Mrs. Oliver up, otherwise I know she'll never get to George and she has to if the plan is to work. "We should think about your photographs soon," I said. Her cheeks went pink, which surprised me. Someone has made her feel bad, I thought, but I couldn't think who she would have told. "It wouldn't take much to make you into a sweetheart," I lied.

She grimaced then. "Forget I ever said anything," she said suddenly, standing up. "No fool like an old fool."

Luckily, just then, Helen Elliott came out of the room, her hair a flurry of white cotton candy and spray.

"You look like a film star," I told her. "Beautiful."

Of course, Helen's a bit stiff to do any actual flirting especially now she's so pally with Catherine, but when I turned back to Mrs. Oliver, I knew I'd timed it just right by the look she was giving me.

"If we were to do something as stupid as have some photographs taken," she said, "no one's to see them, or even to know about them."

"Anything you want," I said. Her look was hungry, just like the one you had, Mo, that first day in my studio when I caught you staring at the photographs on my wall. It's what attracted you to me in the first place.

I knew I'd got her, just as I knew I'd got you that day. Only difference is I've learned my lesson. I'm not going to fall for Mrs. Oliver like I did for you. You only have one heart to give away.

Afterward, I went to see George. We've got so we just knock on each other's doors now without appointments or anything. It makes me laugh thinking how you would have jumped if I'd come around to your front door to call for George.

"I was wondering if you wanted to look at some of my photographs," I said as offhandedly as I could manage. He's hinted several times but I've put him off. Not just because I don't like the idea of it, but I couldn't take the risk of him finding yours. Even, maybe especially, because you're fully dressed. However many times I hide it away, it always seems to rise up to the surface.

He was going through the local newspaper, underlining things so hard I could see he was almost tearing the page. His latest thing is to find spelling and grammar mistakes in the stories and then he writes to the editor to complain. "Now?" he asked.

I suddenly felt tired. "Tomorrow," I said. Although why that should be better than today, I'm sure I don't know. He looked excited.

"I'd be very interested," he said. "Particularly with what you have told me about that period of your life, which is so different from my own experiences. It'll be a useful insight."

Insight indeed. He's like all the others and just wants an ogle at some naked flesh. Still, I'm going to spend the rest of this evening sorting out the photos I want him to see. I'm after the models who have a look of Mrs. Oliver about them. It's all to do with planting seeds, you see. "Does she remind you of someone?" I'll ask. And give him a few more clues until he thinks he's come up with the idea himself. Then I'll give him some ideas about how to talk to women. Perhaps which film stars he could compare them to.

M

90. LETTER FROM GEORGE GRIFFITHS TO BRENDA LEWIS

Dear Mrs. Lewis,

My daughter has suggested I take up some hobbies, so I have decided to organize a Residents Committee to help you with the arduous task of running Pilgrim House. There are many jobs we could take on, and it would be beneficial for residents to feel they were playing an active role in their own care.

Because I am, as you may be aware, the only resident here who has a management background, I would be willing to take on the major share of the organization involved, and I'd be grateful if we could have a meeting at your earliest convenience to discuss this further.

Yours sincerely,
George Griffiths

91. ANSWER PHONE MESSAGE FROM
GEORGE GRIFFITHS TO ANGIE GRIFFITHS

Hello Angie,

This is your father speaking. Have you any hobbies? I ask because Nell is trying to persuade me that they are essential for my mental health. I have decided to play along with her so I am taking a close interest in the local paper and believe I can assist the editor in some improvements he should be making. In addition, I plan action closer to home. Do you remember when our neighbor on Boleyn Drive insisted on parking his car on the pavement, and my campaign, ably assisted by your mother on the administration side, resulted in the offending automobile being towed away by the police? Well, I expect such a victory happening here very soon, although not with parking, of course, as no resident has a car. However, haven't I always said that a principle is a principle. I just need to get the right team together. I hope you are well, this is George Griffiths.

Oh, by the way, if you are still there, I seem to have formed a friendship here with another resident. Your mother would have teased me as she always joked how I wasn't any good at the talking stakes, but it is healthy to form links with people you might not otherwise have come into contact with. It is more than I could have expected as I dwindle into old age and people seem to increasingly ignore our needs. It is a good job I have never seen the point of self-pity. Your father.

92. LETTER FROM FLORENCE OLIVER TO LIZZIE CORN

Dear Lizzie,

You could have bowled me over with a feather when I opened your letter and that old photograph of us fell out. Of course, Susan Reed got hold of it first. She has no idea about keeping some things private. "Ooo," she said, "and who's this?"

"Me and my best friend," I said. "And I'll thank you to keep your marmalade-covered mitts off it."

But she didn't. It was just me and her and BethandKeith in the dining room. "Look at Lady Muck." Susan waved our photograph in the air.

"Let's see," Beth said, taking the photograph carefully, just using the tips of her fingers on the edge so I couldn't really mind. "Oh, Florence," she said then. "You were really glamorous."

And then of course Keith had to have a look, and he nodded away so enthusiastically that Susan had to change her tone. "You looked good, Florence," she admitted, but I could tell it cost her.

"I won't deny I had some style," I said. Because we did, didn't we, pet? Do you remember that time we wore trousers to learn to bicycle? We were the first they'd seen around the camp and people came out of their houses to look. How lucky was I that no one told Graham? I was going to mention about the trousers, but Beth had one of her coughing fits then and Keith was fetching her a glass of water, and Susan was rushing because she had a grandchild coming at nine, so there was no one left to tell.

But then, you will never guess what happened, not in a million sunsets. George came into the room and he took hold of the photograph too. "It's nice," he said, staring at it. "Reminds me of someone, but I can't put a name to her. A film star of the old school, maybe, before all the vulgarity crept in."

I felt like a teenager all over again and I couldn't think of anything to say. Just opened and shut my mouth like a goldfish. Then he handed it back to me. "No milk on the table as per usual," he said. "It really is too bad. Where is that Steve?"

I knew Steve and Sophi would be kissing in the kitchen so when he said someone should do something about the way the meals were run, I nodded enthusiastically to distract him. Then, when he stopped talking for a moment, I made my escape. I took the photograph up to my room and slipped it into an envelope. Then I wrote a note to go with it saying, "This is how I want to look when you take your photographs." I would have liked to have held on to it for a bit longer and think about us a bit more, but I knew I might change my mind, so I just shoved it under Martin's door.

Sophi has lent me her college prospectus. I'm not applying— not that much of a fool—but I like to read through it. You wouldn't guess how many subjects you can study, even Troy's massaging. I slept with it under my pillow last night. Sociology, biology, psychology, history. I wanted them all to come into my dreams. Perhaps I am an old fool.

I'm glad we're friends again. I don't like it when we argue. I could never abide tension of any kind, which is a bit of a joke when you think about Graham. Anyway, time for us to put our thinking caps on and plan Bournemouth. And I want you to tell me all about young Amy's fallen arches. No wonder Laurie doesn't want her doing sports at school, particularly when she gets teased already for being on the plump side.

Yours aye,
Flo

93. EMAIL FROM NELL BAKER TO ANGIE GRIFFITHS

Martin is an absolute dear. Even Robyn says he's "OK," which is five steps up from "Whatever."

He's teaching her to learn poems by heart because apparently you understand the rhythm better that way. I stand in the doorway and just listen to them sometimes. He's picked all of Mum's favorites, and it sends shivers down my spine hearing Robyn say them.

He spent a long time looking at your photograph the other day—the one of you underneath the Eiffel Tower looking up. He didn't say anything, just put his finger up as if he was going to touch your face.

"When's her birthday?" he asked, which surprised me a bit. And when I told him, he turned the photograph on its side and squinted a bit. I suppose he's got a professional interest from when he used to take photographs himself.

94. LETTER FROM MARTIN MORRIS TO MO GRIFFITHS

Dear Mo,

You should have told me. Even if you wanted nothing to do with me, I had a right to know the child was mine. I could see the similarities the minute I picked up the photograph, and then the dates matched exactly. I saw her with you, of course, watched her grow up, but always at such a distance. And I always see better in photographs.

The trouble is I don't know what to do now. And I'm trying not to think less of you. Did George know? Does she know? Did you really feel you had a right to keep that secret from all of us?

Angie. I keep thinking of Angel, and how I used to call you that.

And what did you do to her that was so terrible she went running off to Paris and didn't come back for years? She keeps making excuses even now although George and Nell beg her to come home.

She found out about us, didn't she? Oh Mo. What a mess you made of everything. You must have longed for me to be by your side. My stomach hurts. I feel bits of body I'd forgotten I had. It's as if I'm transforming into something else. A father.

M

95. EMAIL FROM NELL BAKER TO ANGIE GRIFFITHS

What's the big interest in Martin? He only looked at your photograph carefully. Lots of men do that, and you've never made a big thing of it before.

I would say harmless is the best way to describe him, but I'll get Robyn to write a proper description for you if you want. Martin says she has a real gift for characterization. She won't let me see her pieces, of course, but what's new?

"Have you been writing about me?" I asked her. I've never forgotten the time she told the teacher I wore big earrings and played football every Saturday, and this was why James had to leave us. But she said that they'd been looking at the Pilgrims. "As if they are real people with real lives," she said, "and not just a stereotype." She's developed this way of staring at me that always makes me think she has her hands on her hips, although of course she never does. *Fine*, I wanted to say, *well, you go around and take real Dad real shopping every real Thursday like I do.* But I didn't. I just said "fine," like I always do, but I thought she looked a bit hesitant. It's hard to know when to push and when to leave alone. She still won't see James. He's living with the landscape architect now. How come he can find a man, and I can't?

Angie, you're right. I need a real life. But where am I going to find one here in Bedford?

96. LETTER FROM FLORENCE OLIVER TO LIZZIE CORN

Dearest Lizzie,

Why on earth did Troy think going out on a boat would be a treat? I can imagine how worried you were, particularly as Laurie must have told him about Brian's motion sickness. And fancy having to wear those big life jackets. I bet you did panic when the toggles on yours got stuck in the oars. No wonder Amy started crying. I would have done myself.

We are quiet here. Martin has a cold, which means he spends most of his time in his bedroom. You know what men are like with illness. The other day though, I was in the sitting room going through my notes from the Investment Committee when George walked in. I thought he was going to ignore me as per normal but he came over and looked at what I was doing. Of course, I tried to hide the minutes because he would have realized I knew what I was talking about, but he was more interested in how I was laying things out. Before I knew it I'd shown him my files and how I organized everything.

"I could have been a secretary," I told him. Because I could, if Mother hadn't thought it not a suitable job for girls, and then of course Graham didn't want any wife of his working. I thought how Sophi would laugh if I told her that.

"You would have been an excellent one," George said. "Some people have a natural flair for order." And then we arranged a time for another chat about money. A natural flair. I liked that.

Anyway, I went into town with Helen and Lady F this afternoon and have got myself a new red coat for our Bournemouth adventure. Can you see me in it? I was going to go for a beige anorak like normal, but then I was thinking about you and me and us wearing trousers, and I thought, why not? The shop assistant wasn't sure. "It's very bright," she said, but I asked her if she would wear it, and she said yes, so I said, "Well, why should young people be the ones to have all the fun?" She had nothing to reply to that. Nor did Helen and Lady F when I turned up at the bus stop wearing it. You should have seen their faces.

I am blossoming, Lizzie. It's only taken seventy-nine bloody years but it feels good. I miss Martin, though. I got him some oranges in town. I'll take them to him after I've popped this in the letterbox. Young Robyn was here earlier with a note for him. It's just as I told you. All children love Martin. It's as if he can enter their world.

Well, I hope Amy doesn't catch another cold after falling in the river. And her not being able to swim either. Well, at least Troy jumped in and rescued her, and although I'm pleased the water was only knee-high, I can imagine how worried you all were. It doesn't sound like my idea of a fun afternoon at all. There is absolutely no need for us to go on a boat trip in Bournemouth. We shall stay firmly on dry land.

Yours aye,
Flo

97. LETTER FROM MARTIN MORRIS TO ROBYN GRIFFITHS

Dear Robyn,

Thank you for the note. I am surprised you are having second thoughts but you need to think of your mother in these situations. She has told me several times how happy it makes her that you are learning the same poems her own mother loved. And you are the only one who can really look after her at the moment, aren't you?

I don't think it would be best for you to have your poems and stories back either. Although you say that you are now determined to write more nature poems, I would hate for the pieces you wrote about The Pilgrims to be found by unsympathetic readers. Non-writers, such as your mother, could easily misinterpret the exercises you carried out and take offense. I am sure the last thing either of us would want to do is to cause unnecessary anguish. Why don't I continue to look after them for the time being, and we can discuss what we should do when I come around for our usual meeting next week? I will be back in fighting form by then.

In the meantime, do look after yourself,

Martin

98. LETTER FROM MARTIN MORRIS TO MO GRIFFITHS

Dear Mo,

So I have around my chair a number of things that have an association with you: that photograph of you taken at my studio, your copy of *The Mayor of Casterbridge,* a book of John Clare's poems that Robyn and I have been reading and which you always loved, the packet of cornflower seeds stolen from your husband's room and that he has told me since were your favorite flowers, which is why he's upset to have lost them.

It still seems a poor recompense for what you took from me. My own daughter.

But at least this is one thing I am not too late for. You see, the other thing I have in front of me is a letter to your granddaughter. What if I were to put the wrong letter in the wrong envelope and sent Robyn this one instead? It would be such an easy mistake to make and young Robyn would be sure to ask questions. And one thing will lead to another and the truth will come out. To think for all those years I thought I had no power over you, or what we were doing.

M

99. NOTE FROM BRENDA LEWIS TO STEVE JENKINS (ATTACHED TO LETTER 90)

Dear Steve,

George has written this letter about a Residents Committee. Could you organize something just to keep him quiet? I've attached it.

Thanks,
Brenda

100. LETTER FROM FLORENCE OLIVER TO LIZZIE CORN

Dear Lizzie,

No, I am not sure how I would get on with meditating either, although I can see it's nice to sit still and have the kiddies quiet for a bit. You'll have to teach me in Bournemouth, although maybe you'll need a bit of a rest by then. Troy does seem a whirlwind. I bet you wonder what he'll have you doing next.

We are in our own little whirlwind here. "You're very popular all of a sudden," Beth Carter said the other day. She has a bit more time to herself now that Keith has taken up translating *The Odyssey* from the original into English. "Does he know ancient Greek?" I asked Beth, but she said no. He's going through it word by word from an old dictionary he got from a secondhand book-shop apparently. She doesn't care because it takes up all his energy and he spends less time fussing over her. Which is why she has time to notice things like how Martin, George, and I have become quite a little threesome.

So everyone is happy, although when Keith spreads his books out in the sitting room and hushes us, I can tell it annoys George.

Well, everything annoys him really. Apart from Martin. "Are we still up for the seduction then?" I asked Martin the other day, and he said perhaps we'd better put it on hold for the moment because of this Residents Committee. But it's as if Martin's taken the job over for himself. He and George are always in corners having deep chats, and the other night they went off to the pub together without telling me.

"What about my photos?" I asked Martin, not so much because I wanted them as I wanted to be part of it all again.

"We'll do those soon," he said.

But I don't know. Tonight, when the woman from the grocers came to talk about foreign food, I went over to sit with Catherine and Helen on purpose. "Look what the cat's brought in. We're very honored, I'm sure," Helen said, but I bit my tongue. It was only when the woman's wig started to slip and you could see her bald patch that I looked around at where George and Martin were sitting. Martin was open-mouthed, not from the bald patch but as if learning about different cheeses in France was all he ever wanted to know about. Even when the woman passed around this plate of cheese that smelled like Graham's armpits after he'd been on the parade ground, Martin took two chunks.

"And this is definitely what they eat in France?" he asked, and when the woman nodded he crammed them into his mouth.

"How soon is soon?" I'd wanted to ask Martin, but of course I didn't. Graham taught me the importance of waiting.

And then afterward, when Brenda was taking the cheese woman out, Annabel Armstrong stood up and walked into the middle of our circle of chairs. She's been less herself recently even more than usual, but there was no need for Helen to mock. "Aye, aye," she said, "here's the cabaret. More virgins, I expect."

Annabel curtseyed then, held her dress out around her and started to sing. It was a thin warble that felt like you wanted to turn the radio up to hear properly. "Daisy, daisy, give me your answer do . . ."

And of course Helen had to join in. "I'm half crazy." She was winking at us as she sang. She's been unbearable since palling up with Catherine, but to give Lady F her credit, she hushed Helen.

Annabel's little face was all flushed, and she put her hand up to her heart.

"All for the love of you," she warbled, and then blow me down but Martin didn't join in. "I can't afford a carriage," he sang, and because he didn't seem to be teasing her, the rest of us joined in too. "But you'll look sweet, upon the seat . . ."

And at the end, when we all bellowed out together, " . . . made for two," Annabel curtseyed again before going up to Martin.

"Thief," she said, and then she walked out of the room.

I was as quiet as the rest of them then, not sure what had happened, but before anyone could say anything, Brenda bustled back.

"Well, that was a very nice talk," she said. "So interesting." We were still looking at each other, a bit shell-shocked. "I do believe she's tired you all out," Brenda said.

For some reason, I looked at George. *I'll punch you if you say anything about Annabel,* I was thinking. But he just shook his head. "She was very stimulating," he said. "And now it's up the rolling hills of Bedfordshire for me." And we all got up and left, although Brenda said she was planning to make us an extra cup of good British tea as a treat. She doesn't always let us drink tea so near bedtime but I suppose she felt a bit put out by the speaker's comment that French coffee was better.

But now I'm sitting here writing this, and I wonder why George didn't say anything because it wasn't like him not to spill the beans on anything out of the ordinary. It's a mystery, and you know me and mysteries, Lizzie. I need to find a way of getting to the bottom of it all.

Yours aye,

Flo

101. LETTER FROM MARTIN MORRIS TO MO GRIFFITHS

Dear Mo,

I went out and planted your cornflower seeds today. There's a spot around a bench here that I think you would like. I nearly toppled over when I was leaning forward to make sure they were pushed in properly. It's one of the perils of getting old. You lose your sense of balance and forget how far you can go before you won't be able to get back again.

I'm still going around to teach Robyn at her home. She's a good girl, just wants to please her mother. She mostly works away on her own, while I look through Nell's things. Of course, I never sent her your letter, Mo, but I did ask her about you the other day. She didn't want to tell me at first, but I started talking about those funny poems she wrote about us all at Pilgrim House until she opened up a bit more. "She was kind, but quiet," Robyn said. "Granddad mostly did the talking for her, but I think she always got on with Auntie Angie more than Mum. That's what Mum says anyway."

Of course, you preferred Angie because of me, but that doesn't mean that Nell's not important to me now. They're becoming my family as much as yours. And when we get Angie back here, then we'll all be together. As we should have been.

George didn't deserve any of you. He and I went to the pub the other day and I asked him about Angie. He didn't say anything about her, but just started going on about this important mystery job that keeps her in France. "So you speak to her often?" I asked, and his eyes didn't even start to water. Muttered something about talking to a machine. "So when was the last time you saw her?" I asked, and he said she'd come back briefly for your funeral but went away again straight after.

"You could see her," I said. "You could get her back here."

"No," he said, and he did this straightening his shoulders thing he does. As if someone's shoving a stick down his back. I could tell it annoyed him, having to admit something in his life wasn't going the way it should.

"I could help you," I said. "All you need to do is to stop telling your girls what to do, and praise them even if you're not sure they deserve it. Especially then."

He said he'd think about it, but that he'd always been unsure about praising too much. It builds up false hopes, apparently, and he'd always thought the inside was more important than the outside. He doesn't let up, does he? Mrs. Oliver says she's changed her mind, and that he's a good man, but I wouldn't know about that. Good men, in my experience, never win in the end.

Talking of which, I am afraid I had to go in and talk to Brenda about Annabel Armstrong. I have managed to pass her insults off as part of her sickness, but things are getting a bit too serious now for anything to spoil my plans.

M

102. LETTER FROM GEORGE GRIFFITHS TO BRENDA LEWIS

Dear Brenda,

I had a visit from Steve Jenkins today to talk about the Residents Committee. There is absolutely no point having such a committee if it is to be run by a member of the staff. It should be a chance for residents to speak freely about points that concern them. I am also disappointed that you delegated such an important job to a junior employee. I have been talking to several of the other residents about this matter, and you have left us no option but to take matters into our own hands.

Yours sincerely,
George Griffiths

103. ANSWER PHONE MESSAGE FROM GEORGE GRIFFITHS TO ANGIE GRIFFITHS

Hello Angie,

This is your father. It is Thursday afternoon, and I have just come back from a walk around the park with the other male resident here. There are some daffodils already out along the edges, but they had been trampled by the boys playing football. A parkkeeper was attending to some mulching at the far side, and although I was tempted to complain, I came to the conclusion that ball games are all part of growing up. I hope the weather is clement with you. Do keep in touch. I always enjoy your cards and the photographic insight into another culture.

Your father

104. EMAIL FROM NELL BAKER TO ANGIE GRIFFITHS

Yes, I've noticed Dad has been a bit strange recently too. Not only did he thank me for visiting the other day but he even tried to make a joke when we went to the optician. Every time she asked a question, he said "eye." The trouble was she was Scottish and thought he was teasing her. He didn't notice her face getting redder and redder.

At least he didn't complain about the fact she was a woman. Remember when he'd only see male opticians, dentists, and stuff? Perhaps he's mellowing. It can happen.

And as for Martin, I don't know why you keep going on about him. Hand on heart, he's absolutely fine. I might not be the best judge of men, but I'm sure about this one.

Even Dad likes him. And Robyn.

105. LETTER FROM FLORENCE OLIVER TO LIZZIE CORN

Dear Lizzie,

So we are all a little sad here. Annabel Armstrong was moved to the hospital last night. We could all see it coming, but it's still a shock when it happens. Three residents have left since I've been here. After the first time, I kept thinking it may be me next. I guess we all did. But this time, it's Annabel.

I've noticed we are all bowing our heads a little when we walk past her room. The door's been shut all day, but before lunch I could hear Steve and Brenda in there chatting and then the sound of the vacuum cleaner. Helen said they'd be getting ready for the next person, but as Lady F pointed out, people do sometimes come back. It's just not all that usual. Tom Pardoe didn't, after all. We were still waiting for him when Martin appeared in his room.

It's funny how you learn things about someone after they've gone. Annabel has two sons apparently. She never mentioned them so we all thought she was childless. Barren. That's the proper term. It's what Graham used to call me, and it still hurts. It feels like such a manly thing to be. Like a baron, all German mustaches and baton swirling. As if I wasn't a proper woman. Which of course in many ways I'm not. Don't be kind and jump in. I know what you think about women and motherhood.

Anyway, one of the sons lives just up the road. He was the one who came around to pick up her things after she'd gone to the hospital.

Beth Crosbie and I watched him from the sitting room. He seemed normal. The sort of man you'd pass in the street and would expect to keep in touch with his mother. So how did we never know about him? And who was it, if it wasn't for him, that she would sing "Daisy Daisy" and all those other nursery rhymes for?

And if there are two sons, then there had to be a Mister Annabel too, which comes as more of a shock. I always thought she might have been untouched. She was so much like a small girl in her flowered dresses and straight hair. I wonder about him now, was he kind to her or was he harsh? It's as if, here, we all go back to the beginning when none of that need matter.

I'm writing this in the sitting room now. We're nearly a full house. Beth is drowsing on one of the chairs opposite while, in the corner, Keith plows on with his research. He sticks his tongue out when he works. Doesn't just let it fall, but actually holds the tip of it between his thumb and forefinger. I want to ask Beth if that's something he's always done, or if it's a strange new habit he's picked up. But she doesn't pay him any attention, so I think that yes, he will have always done that and maybe it annoyed her at one time but now she's used to it. I suppose it's these little things about people that we come to love or hate. Sometimes both.

Helen's sitting a little closer to Lady F than she normally does as I write this, but they're not playing their usual game of Scrabble. And Martin and George have disappeared. They've gone to Martin's room, I should imagine, because they spend hours in there. And so we wait to hear whether Annabel will come back to us or not. Somehow if there are plans afoot tonight, then I'm too tired for them.

Yours aye,
Flo

106. LETTER FROM MARTIN MORRIS TO MO GRIFFITHS

Dear Mo,

I swear I can hear Marta, the au pair, crying in her bed at night. It comes through the wall and echoes around my room until I want to scrabble through the bricks and shake her back into happiness. Or at least into her way of "being."

And then the next morning, I go back to my chair at the window and watch her in the garden with the boys. They've taken to including her in their games. She's either the princess they have to tie up before rescuing, or she is the foreign witch they need to capture and then tie up.

I have told them they can have one of my cameras if they play nicely with her.

"But you wouldn't know if we did or not, would you?" the first boy says. He's the loudest, but the second boy is the cleverest, I think.

"I know everything," I told him. "I know, for instance, where you've planted your treasure."

They both gave a start then, but while the first boy looked at the base of the tree where I'd seen them digging the other day, the second boy looked up at the house, trying to see if I could have been watching them.

A camera is a camera, though. I think Marta will be spared some of their rope.

M

107. EMAIL FROM NELL BAKER TO ANGIE GRIFFITHS

Dad is now officially worrying me.

I'd gone in to Pilgrim House to tell him about Martin and Robyn's poetry classes. She wanted me to tell Dad. And she's right. You wait until you have the little nipper and it starts telling you how to behave.

Anyway, I got caught up in some traffic on the way there so I was all of about eight minutes late. I expected to find one of Dad's notes, you know the ones: "I'm very disappointed," but he was standing there instead. Smiling. "I'm sorry," I started, but he just shook his head. And then he suggested we go for a walk because it was a beautiful day. He was talking about how one of the residents had been taken to the hospital, and we walked around the yard twice before he even mentioned Robyn. He didn't complain about her though, just asked how her poetry was getting on. Of course that's when I should have said something about the lessons, but Dad said he'd never seen the point of poetry, but different courses for different horses, eh?

It was the "eh?" that put me off. Since when has Dad ever questioned anything?

But before I could say anything, he said he'd been thinking about me and he only wanted to know whether I would be interested in letting either Sandra or Gill—they're the hairdressers who go in to Pilgrim House—do my hair. He even said he'd arrange it as a treat for me. I pretended I had to go to a meeting and I ran to the car, Angie, just to get away. But then I had to sit there for a few minutes catching my breath. Since when has Dad ever thought about hairdressers or how we look? Can you imagine him thinking about Mum's hair? You need to seriously think about coming over here. Fast.

How is the baby? Have you told the father yet? Whatever happens, he needs to know.

108. LETTER FROM CLAUDE BICHOURIE TO ANGELA GRIFFITHS

Ma petite,

What on earth could be so urgent that I need to break my family holiday to come back to Paris? Maybe you are missing me, but if so, then you will need to be patient just a little bit longer. I long for you too, but we both know there are rules for these things. And consequences for breaking them. Here is a check for you to buy something pretty, or take your girlfriends out for supper and complain about us. Your naughty absent men.

Until soon,
Claude

109. LETTER FROM MARTIN MORRIS TO MO GRIFFITHS

Dear Mo,

He's insatiable, this husband of yours. Every spare minute we have now and he's on at me to look at the photographs. I get them out, and just watch him while he looks.

"They really are very tasteful." He always sounds as if he's surprised when he says this, but of course the photographs are. Times were different then, but it's as if he needs to be persuaded that he's not committing some sin by looking through them. I wonder if he's a little disappointed too because I won't tell him anything about the girls. The way he talks sometimes makes me think he suspects we had ourselves one long party that he missed out on. As if he'd have been invited if we had.

I asked him straight the other day, "Did you ever play around?" He winced. It was as if I'd hit him.

"I think that's possibly between me and my conscience." He adjusted his tie as he spoke. If he'd have pulled it any tighter, it would have throttled him.

"So you did," I replied. I tried not to look surprised, or too interested.

"No!" He almost shouted. I raised an eyebrow at him. He was sitting there holding a photograph of Anita, the little Spanish girl who lived above her parents' restaurant. I'd got her to bring in this ornate fan from home and she was peeping out from behind it. "It's my mother's," she kept saying, and laughing. That was a good shoot, but she came just the once. Although they never said as much, for some of these girls coming to me was their last fling before marriage. As if they wanted a record of another them, not the dutiful wife they were bound to turn into, out there in the world.

I have learned to keep silent with George, so I said nothing until he started to turn Anita's photograph this way and that so energetically I wanted to hold out my hand for him to give it back.

"I may have gone shopping once," he said, "with a lady who was not my wife."

Shopping! Well, call the police, why don't you? It was all I could do not to laugh but he was red-faced. I bit my tongue.

"It was Maureen's friend who had the idea," George said. "It was to buy a dress for Maureen's fortieth birthday. And the whole thing was to be a surprise. We met at lunchtime and went to a department store together."

I could just picture old George rushing out from Flanders, Flanders and Flanders, or whatever it was his accountancy office was called. All flustered and looking around to see if anyone was noticing him. And you oblivious at home, love. Thinking of me.

"She was quite different from Maureen," George was saying. I went alert then because he so rarely talked about you. I wanted him to carry on, but he was talking about this friend of yours. "All bubbly and giggly. A real daredevil. She was always going on about living in America and becoming a film star. I had never seen what Maureen saw in her before our shopping trip."

I could, because I suddenly guessed who that friend might be. Trisha. I couldn't imagine you having more than one friend who would be a daredevil. No harm in that, but you were always such a safety-first woman. Was I your only reckless gesture? There's a certain pleasure in the way I'm able now to put pieces of your life together like a jigsaw. Now, as George talked, I could even picture Trisha waiting for him, twiddling those long pearls she wore and laughing. You never liked her giggle, did you? But I think most men did. I did, and I could tell from the way he was smiling now that George did too. He'd certainly learned to see what you saw in her.

"We looked at several dresses, and Pat—that was her name, Maureen's friend." He looked across at me and I nodded. Pat, Trisha. Maureen, Mo. It made sense. "Well, she kept teasing me about my choices. Said Maureen was going to be forty, not sixty."

I'd have dressed you in white every day, love. I'd have had simple shifts made for you that you could just slip on. Colored scarves to drape over your shoulder so you could change your look from moment to moment. A red silk dressing gown. A pair of blue Chinese slippers so you would feel you were floating.

"And then she picked out this dress. I stared at it. Maureen in that? I thought she must be joking, but she wasn't. This is the one, she kept saying. Maureen will love it.

"So I said yes. Just like that. Although I told her she'd have to try it on for me first. I don't know what came over me."

I did. I'd seen him look through my box of photographs enough times by now to know he had more fire beneath his surface than he let on. I was trying to think what happened to those photographs of Trisha I took that first day.

"So she went into the changing room with the dress and I waited outside. It's not something I've ever done before so I didn't know what to do. There was another man sitting there waiting too and we smiled at each other. Women, we seemed to say, and I thought I could get used to this, but then Pat came out and I moved across so the other man couldn't keep staring at her in the way he was."

George's face was transformed. It was as if someone had smoothed all the lines away. He was looking out of the window of my room as if he could see someone standing there.

"She looked so beautiful, Martin. Like she was lit up. And she did this twirl for me."

He held up his hands then, and I had a sudden panic he was going to stand up and twirl right in the middle of my room, but he let them drop. As if his fingers had suddenly become heavy.

"And the shop assistant came up and said to me, 'Don't you think this suits your wife?' 'Yes,' I said. 'Yes, yes. We'll have it.' But it was only after, when Pat went back in to get changed, that I realized I'd lied about Pat being my wife and she hadn't corrected me either."

His shoulders slipped down his back, like wings dropping. I could imagine his stupid embarrassment. "But you got the dress?" I asked. My mouth was dry. I was thinking about that time in the studio, when you and Trisha came for the first time. You and me together, when Trisha was in the changing room. I didn't want George to ruin that memory with this silly shopping story.

"Yes," he said. "It was red silk. Very inappropriate. Maureen gasped when she opened the box, but she wore it. For my sake, I suppose, because after the party, I never saw it again."

Red silk. My red silk dressing gown. Pat would have remembered that. And so would Maureen.

"And Pat?" I asked. "Did you and her go out again?"

"We never spoke about it," George said. "In fact, we didn't ever find ourselves alone again. Even at the party, we stayed apart. It felt deliberate, and afterward she didn't come around so much. Much later I asked Maureen about her and she said she didn't see her anymore. My wife had a way of talking sometimes that stopped all further discussion."

When George was telling this story, I kept thinking how easy it would have been if he'd had a proper love affair with Pat so I could feel angry.

Anyway, that was your husband's big secret. After he'd gone, I found the photograph of Anita on my bed. He'd torn it in half somewhere during the telling of his tale. I've taped it up, but it will never be the same again.

It must have been just after your fortieth birthday that you moved into the bigger house, on the other side of town. Were you trying to get away from me? I thought it was just a step up, but now I wonder. Pat must have known how the red dress would have reminded you of me. It must have been like I was there, at the party. You must have thought it was a sign when you opened the unexpected present from your husband. Of course, you'd have known by then that you'd never get rid of me.

M

110. ANSWER PHONE MESSAGE FROM
       NELL BAKER TO ANGIE GRIFFITHS

Angie! More flowers. Everyone stared when Mark, that security officer, brought them into the office. He said that someone must love me, and I blurted out it was my sister. Of course, he winked at me again. "Nice when families are close," he said. And then for some reason I asked if he had any sisters. He was standing there in his security officer uniform clutching your huge bunch of flowers that I didn't take from him or ask him to put down or anything.

"Yes," he said. "Three."

"Gosh," I said. "Then you must know all about women."

I could die. *Gosh, you must know all about women.*

This is all your fault. Nice flowers, though. And thanks for the good luck wishes. I feel pathetic to be so nervous about a talk in an old people's home. Mark asked why you were sending me flowers so I told him, and he offered to help me carry all the stuff I'm taking for the talk. Don't say anything. Nothing at all.

111. LETTER FROM FLORENCE OLIVER TO LIZZIE CORN

Dear Lizzie,

I am sorry Annabel's departure upset you so much, but I suppose we get used to such things in here. Annabel's room has been left with her things in, and for the moment that is enough for us to keep on hoping.

Life goes on anyway, whether we like it or not.

Last night, George's daughter, Nell, came to talk to us about trend forecasting. It was quite a palaver because she had brought lots of things with her. "Are you moving in?" Keith asked her. "We'll have to do an age check because I think you might be a bit too young." She even had a policeman to help her carry them in. "Hello hello hello," Keith said. "The strong arm of the law." He's got a bit tiring since he started his translating project, to tell you the truth, because he seems to feel he has to be doubly noisy to make up for being busy. And he's here more and more. I keep looking to George to sort it out, but somehow he doesn't do as much complaining as he used to. It puts more pressure on the rest of us.

Anyway, eventually Nell was all set up. Although when she started talking, I thought we were going to have a catastrophe like the sweaty gasman all over again. She stumbled and stuttered and couldn't get any words out. She always has such an air of seeking approval about her, so I didn't dare look at her father. I'm ex-trasensitive because of Graham, of course, but I could hear George harrumphing at the back, and Brenda kept doing her "very nice" bit in the way she does when things aren't going quite how she wants them to be.

Nell had a laptop with her but none of us could see what we were supposed to be seeing on it, so she kept tilting it this way and that in a manner that made us dizzy. And then Helen got worried that the flashing lights would bring about one of Lady F's headaches, so Nell had to give up on it.

She stood there, looking at us all and I thought she might burst into tears. Robyn stood up and started walking to the front. She's too protective of her mother, that one. The others say it's nice to see, but I always did what my mother said and look what happened to me. I could have had a desk job, had people call me "Miss" and kept clean. Sophi tells me I could have aimed even higher, but an office would have been lovely. Sophi wants to work in "the field," which makes us both chuckle.

Anyway, back to Nell. Before Robyn could reach her, Nell opened her mouth. "My mother was a marvelous cook," she said. "If I shut my eyes and think of her now, I see her in the kitchen. She used to wear a red-and-white-dotted apron, and my sister, Angie, and I would rush back from school every day to see what cake she had made us.

"Date and walnut loaf, coffee cake, banana bread, Victoria sponges oozing with jam and lightly dusted with sugar. She'd pretend not to have time to wash up the bowls so we could lick them clean."

Robyn sat down in the front row, next to BethandKeith. You

could tell he'd stopped thinking of what jokes he could make and was sitting forward, his chin cupped in his hands. I was leaning forward too. We all were. It wasn't just that her voice was light and we had to strain to hear. None of us had baked or even eaten a homemade cake for years. I could feel my hands twitching as if they wanted to be stirring the bowl. Nell was quite different from the bread lady, or the sugar-petal woman who wouldn't let us touch. I wished Annabel could have been there. It would have soothed her nicely.

"Shepherd's pie, meatballs, bangers and mash and gravy. Roast beef with horseradish sauce on Sundays. Rhubarb custard, apple and black currant crumble. Yorkshire pudding."

I looked at Nell's policeman. He had his eyes shut. Ay-oop, I thought, there's a man falling in love. "But my daughter here," Nell pointed at Robyn who I guessed would be blushing if she wasn't wearing so much white makeup, "she doesn't know about any of these. I don't cook for her, the way my mother did for me. This is because of the way our lives are all changing."

Get back to the food, I wanted to shout. I was surprised at the rage I felt with Nell for changing the subject. I was thinking of the meals my mother had prepared for me when I was still at home. You and I both tried our best in our little army kitchens but it was never the same. Remember how we would rush in and out of each other's kitchens exchanging eggs and sugar and family recipes, but I could still never get anything quite right for Graham. I don't think I ever told you how he once threw a plate of roast across the room because the gravy was lumpy. It dripped down the walls but he wouldn't let me clear it up. I had to watch it instead just so he could point out each lump to me. It was almost a relief to wake up the next morning and see it still there, to have to work extra hard to scrub it off before Graham came down. I needed to suffer in order to make a fresh start somehow.

So I wanted to hear about how it was done properly. I wished I knew what George was thinking. Would he be proud or would he be sad, missing this wife of his? No wonder he gets sore sometimes, being in here and putting up with the food we get.

Battenberg cake. That's what I remember Mum making for very special times. We called it window cake because it had those four little squares. Like looking through a window at what the rich children ate every day. When I was in service in Biddleborough, the kiddies there used to have cake at teatime. We would finish off what they'd left over for our supper. Our favorite one had walnuts on top. If we'd worked well that day, cook would let us have a walnut each, although usually someone had picked them all off before it came back to us.

But I'm rambling now. It was a lovely talk Nell gave us. She even showed these little silver packets they took up into space with whole meals in them. She asked us whether we thought children in the future would be having pills instead of food. "Like us now," a voice said, and we all turned around because it was Beth speaking. She never normally speaks when Keith's there. Or when he's not. He was beaming, turning his head from side to side as if to tell us all it was his wife making a joke this time. I wasn't the only one who laughed extra loudly. Having a noisier Beth filled up the vacant space left by Annabel.

It was only then that I noticed Martin had gone. I guess all the talk of domestic bliss wasn't really his cup of tea, but the rest of us clapped and clapped when Nell finished. "That was very nice," Brenda kept saying, but this time I think she meant it. And Robyn hugged her mum while the policeman put everything back in the boxes, and when Brenda said, "Shall we have a cup of tea?" Beth made another joke. "Will we have cake with it?" she said, and everyone laughed again. Even George.

But here's a funny thing. Robyn came and sat next to me

while we had our cuppa. You get used to her face and grumpy manner, just as you must have got used to Troy's skirts by now, pet. Anyway, we were sitting there, nice and quietly, when she said to me, "I'm going to get a tattoo. Did it hurt when you got yours done?"

I stared at her. "Tattoo?" I asked, and she nodded. "I haven't got one, love," I said. "Whatever gave you that idea?" She wouldn't say and although we had a giggle about it, I could see her looking puzzled. I told her to talk to Steve about tattoos. Have I told you he's got LOVE written on one hand and HATE on the other? "Which will it be today?" we tease him now. "Is Sophi getting all your love and are we left with hate?" Even Lady F joins in. After all, we're old enough to get used to most things after a while.

"But Susan Reed was in the circus, wasn't she?" Robyn asked. Oh, I had to bring out my hankie again then because I was laughing so much, and Brenda called over to find out what was so funny. I was going to tell but I caught Robyn's hurt expression and just shook my head at Brenda. "No, love," I whispered to Robyn. "Susan Reed was a dental assistant before she got married." I looked across at where Susan was stirring her tea and blowing into it the way she does like a frustrated walrus, and I had to bite my tongue from going off again. Imagine her on a tightrope. And so today was a good day here. Before I went upstairs to my room, I said to George, "You must be proud of your girl," and he said he was, without even mentioning the other one and how much better she did everything. I think we all went to bed dreaming of cakes. We shall have tea and cakes in Bournemouth, darling. You and me. Just sweet things. Sugar and spice.

Yours aye,
Flo

112. **NOTE FROM ROBYN BAKER TO**
NELL BAKER (LEFT ON KITCHEN TABLE)

Dear Mum,

You were supercool last night. I would rather have a mother like you than any homemade cake. You are spicier than a ginger slice, softer than a Victoria sponge, and nuttier than a fruitcake.

Only joking about the last one, but not about the rest. You make me very proud. I hope when I am older, I can be like you.

Love ya,

R

P.S. I like your new boyfriend!!!!

113. **NOTE FROM MARTIN MORRIS TO FLORENCE OLIVER**
(SLIPPED UNDER FLORENCE'S DOOR)

If you would really like some photographs taken, come to my room at 2 p.m. on Wednesday. As you have said yourself, we will tell no one about this.

Martin

114. **LETTER FROM MARTIN MORRIS TO MO GRIFFITHS**

Dear Mo,

I can't remember the last photograph I took. Or the very last one, at least. But it should have been special. A fanfare. It should have been the shot that made me put down my camera and say I have captured Woman here. I have done enough. What it shouldn't be is just a blur.

Did I even have film in the camera? There were times when I didn't bother to develop the shots. People stopped asking me; even Sam gave up on me. Mind, it was all changing so quickly then and the big boys were moving in. He had to protect his position before Frank Bradley had everything sewn up. Amateurs like me just got in the way. It was some months after you left, I remember, when every day crept into the next one, each one making the studio seem dingier and dingier. And me too, I shouldn't wonder.

The girls didn't forget me, though. After Mahad brought me home from the hospital, one of them would pop around. I'd never know when, and I never knew who it would be, but I'd still be conscious enough to register their little moment of hesitation before they stepped over the threshold and started bustling. Why do women always bustle when they're not sure what to do? And then they start telling you what to do. "Martin, you should really . . . " It's supposed to be for your own sake. But it never is. It's to stop you making them feel uncomfortable. They need you to prove they've not failed in the caring stakes. "Martin, you should really take my photograph." So I would. They'd slip off their clothes behind the curtain just like they used to. "How do you want me?" they'd ask. And we'd do all the poses they'd done before. The look over their shoulder, or the one where they were surprised when doing housework. Even in my half-dazed state I could tell they were humoring me.

So I gave it up as much for their sake as mine. I put down my camera, along with my dreams, and I just lay on my bed. I didn't answer the door for two whole weeks. Mahad would leave a newspaper, pint of milk, and a loaf of bread on my doorstep every morning. I'd take them back to my mattress on the floor, and soon I'd be swimming in a nest of newsprint and crumbs. One day I even woke up to find I'd become a photograph. A front page shot of some politician picking up rubbish had imprinted itself on my naked belly. I couldn't even be bothered to rub it off.

Funnily enough, it was Mahad who got me moving again. My old enemy. "Hey you, fat ass." He knocked on my door one day and started shouting. "I need someone to take care of the till for just five minutes."

I never knew whether he did it in the spirit of friendship or as some kind of great victory over the bad man upstairs, but I wouldn't be surprised if it wasn't a bit of both. Probably one of the girls had gone in and told him they were worried. He'd have ignored the girl, he always did, but he'd have taken the message onboard in that inscrutable way of his.

And then one short session behind the till led to another, and another, and soon it was taken for granted that I'd be on early to sort out the papers for the paperboys and -girls. I handed the news out to commuters too bleary-eyed to notice my own lack of focus, until by lunchtime I could go back to bed and drink.

I suppose Mahad kept me on because, even on my worst days, I didn't miss a morning. Every two weeks he would force me to clear out my empty bottles into boxes he'd take to the dump. He wouldn't say anything, just sat in his car and hooted his horn until I brought them down. I was lucky to find someone who would make no judgments, not even as, slowly, my life closed down into the four walls of my studio, the routine of the shop downstairs, and the days I got to watch you.

So it hurts to find that, while I was suffering all this, you were cooking away without a care in the world. I thought when I came here that I was going to find out things that would color in the gaps so I could go to my end finally able to take you in my arms and the years we'd missed out on would just dissolve. But I've found the opposite. Even George was busy taking other women shopping while you were stuffing my own daughter with food. It doesn't seem fair to me.

Mahad means goodness, you know. He told me that once, when the two of us were sitting behind the counter of that newsagent, sipping that sweet tea he loved. "English builder's tea," he said once. "The blood that ran through the veins of the empire, and now mine. Not yours, though. You have something more evil in yours, I think." We were watching the rain fall on the street outside, a few people rushing past under their umbrellas, and no one coming in. I suppose his parents hoped for something different when they called their son "goodness," but they'd been right in their way. Who are any of us to say what was good and what was . . . not good. Sometimes just surviving is enough.

Marta, the Polish girl next door, is leaving. "She's going back home," the boys said. "And good riddance." But I'll miss her. There are times at night when I can coincide my breathing exactly to match her sobs. It's things like that which can make you less lonely. I'm just sorry she didn't see it that way when I told her about the breathing but there was no need for her to look so frightened.

Cakes, eh? Let them eat cake. And I suppose you thought that was the solution to everything. Your own particular brand of goodness. It was never going to be enough, Mo. Not when you were starving yourself.

M

115. ANSWER PHONE MESSAGE FROM
GEORGE GRIFFITHS TO ANGIE GRIFFITHS

Dear Angie, this is your father speaking. I was just wondering if you remembered the cake your mother made you for your ninth birthday. It was in the shape of the Eiffel Tower. You had seen a picture of Paris in one of those art magazines your mother was always buying, and you couldn't stop going on about it. Her cake was a work of love. She spent all night on the icing, even though I told her several times not to bother. I have often wondered if this is what gave you the idea of going to Paris. Anyway, it's late now. I have got out of bed to ring you and the hall floorboards are cold even against my slippers. Perhaps we could forget I rang, but I couldn't stop thinking about that cake. I know relations between your mother and yourself were strained at the end, but I hope you think about the good things she did for you too sometimes. This is your father who loves you.

116. EMAIL FROM NELL BAKER TO ANGIE GRIFFITHS

Well, I did my Pilgrim House talk, Angie, but I was terrible. I stuttered, and stammered, and couldn't remember anything, so I just ran through some of the recipes you'd written down for me. I even talked about bangers and mash and gravy. Can you imagine? To cap it all, I ended up crying because I don't cook good food for Robyn, like Mum did for us. Everyone was kind after, but Dad kept staring at me. I'll probably get a report soon about how I could have improved my talk.

Mark came back home with us later to help carry the stuff I'd taken. He stood in the kitchen while Robyn went on and on about how good I'd been. I tried to give him some money as a thank-you for helping me, but he just laughed. Said I should take him out for lunch one time. As if I could. Imagine what people at work would say if I went out with the security guard. Dad seems to think he's a policeman so I haven't corrected him. At least he'll think that's a proper job.

"Your mum sounded lovely," Mark said.

"She just did what all mum's did then," I replied. "It's different now."

But then Robyn surprised me. "Mum's got a great job," she said. "I'm really proud of her."

I wanted Mark to go away then so I could ask Robyn if that was true. Even when she was younger, it was always James and her going off into huddles talking together about his job and houses and the environment, while I just felt guilty juggling my boring old work with looking after her.

But then Mark started asking me about what I did tucked away in my cubicle, and why trend forecasting mattered, and how we did it. So I told him. Even though he kept asking questions, by the time I eventually got to bed I was kicking myself. I hadn't let him get a word in edgewise.

It was because I hadn't talked to anyone properly for so long. I wish I could be a bit more mysterious like you. I'm going to let Dad's hairdresser do my hair. Be a girl for once. Where's the harm in that?

117. LETTER FROM FLORENCE OLIVER TO LIZZIE CORN

Dear Lizzie,

There's no fool like an old fool. I am going to take a step over to the dark side and I'm not sure if I'll be able to get back. Having these photographs taken doesn't seem like fun anymore, but somehow I can't say no, Lizzie. It's as if I'd be saying no to the part of me that has never had the chance to shine.

I will let you know how it goes, but I shan't send you a copy. I don't even want to see them myself.

Write to me about what we'll do in Bournemouth. Tell me about the games of cards we'll play, the teas we'll have. Tell me about the cakes.

Don't shun me after. I don't know why I feel the need to say this to you, but I do.

Flo

118. LETTER FROM MARTIN MORRIS TO ROBYN BAKER

Dear Robyn,

Thanks for your note advising me that you intend to tell your mother about the way I apparently "prowl around your house," and yes, if you really want our meetings to stop and for me to give you your stories back, then I will bow to your request. But there are certain things you might like to consider first.

In my "prowlings" one day, I came across a small box on a shelf in the basement. It was behind your school files, and at the bottom of a shoebox full of old paints and craft materials. I am always interested in secrets, but imagine my surprise when I looked inside and found photographs of your father along with some poems about how much you miss him. I took the liberty of slipping one in my pocket. The last thing I would want is for your mother to find it and get upset.

As for Mrs. Oliver's tattoo, I have no idea where you got that information from. I have to admire your rich imagination. I am just a humble photographer. I record events, rather than make them up.

I will come to your home on Monday as usual, and you can let me know what you would like me to do.

Yours sincerely,
Martin

119. LETTER FROM MARTIN MORRIS TO MO GRIFFITHS

Dear Mo,

I will be sad when my escapades into Nell's life are over. She is quite different from you. You were such a little homebody, weren't you? All tidy rooms and sparkling windows. Remember when you painted your front room that bright yellow? I was walking past your house one night when I looked up and saw you standing there. I could have gone over and knocked on the window, but I didn't. I just watched you. The way you put your hand up to the wall and stroked it. And then you came over to the window and I couldn't breathe, thinking that at last you would see me and come out. You didn't, though. Someone must have come into the room because you turned your head away from me as you shut the curtains. First one half of you was cut off from me, and then the other. It was like losing a limb. In fact, it was several days at least before I could summon up the energy to come back to your street.

Anyway, I have gathered enough information about Nell for now. Robyn has taken to going up to sit in her bedroom and leaves me to it so I have had lots of opportunities for research. I have acquired another photograph of you and one of Angie. Thanks to a lesson from the librarian about using the computer, I have even read Nell's emails to her sister. I am surprised she uses no password, but at least I now know how she finds her father difficult and has no idea she is falling in love herself. You, dear, she talks about surprisingly little; but both girls discuss me. I am, apparently, a lifesaver. Although it seems Nell feels she has little life to save.

So I shall leave my visits for a while. I won't tell Robyn my decision because I need her to keep alert. If she is any bit of the girl I hope she is, then I expect developments soon. If anything, I am disappointed she has put up with my behavior for so long.

Meanwhile I have plans for this afternoon. It is time for a special photography session I have planned for a while. I need to prepare myself. My model, I anticipate, will need more help than I am used to giving in order to produce a pleasing effect.

M

120. ANSWER PHONE MESSAGE FROM
GEORGE GRIFFITHS TO ANGIE GRIFFITHS

Hello Angie,

It is very quiet here. I don't know where everyone is. I'm just ringing because I still can't stop thinking about your mother's cooking. It's just that I didn't really tell her enough how much I appreciated her. And then Nell gave this talk and it was as if your mother was standing up in front of me, saying "Look at me, look at everything I did for you," and I was ashamed. Do you think she resented how I took her for granted? You knew her better than all of us. Please tell me a little about your mother. I should like to know her better.

Your father

121. LETTER FROM FLORENCE OLIVER TO LIZZIE CORN

Dear Lizzie,

No, you were right to tell me off. I have got so wound up in myself recently that I forget about you, and what a good friend you are.

But then you do something like send me that pretty white cotton handkerchief, and I know that you understand me completely. It was a gentle gift. That's the best word I can think of for it. I hold it up to my face, and I feel soothed. It even smells of lavender, and can I trace a touch of pinewood in there too?

In the big house, when I was working in service, the cook used to brew up a potion we'd decant into bottles to use on the linen before ironing. It was a mixture of lavender and rose petals, and I used to dream what it would be like to sleep on those sheets. I'd beg to be allowed to press them. Once I took a white sheet and wound it around me, around and around. I shut my eyes and for the first time, since leaving home, I felt secure. But of course, I couldn't stay swaddled like that forever, and a couple of months after, I met Graham. Briefly, in his uniform and the way everyone thought him such a good catch, he made me feel as safe.

And now you send me just the right thing to soothe me. Something for a lady, you wrote. I cried when I read that. Thank you, Lizzie.

I shall tell you how the photography session went in my next letter. Not just now, if you don't mind. In the meantime, will you write me a long newsy letter with details of all your family? Reading the classics together sounds very nice, but for a free spirit, Troy seems very dictatorial.

Yours aye,
Flo

122. EMAIL FROM NELL BAKER TO ANGIE GRIFFITHS

Hi Angie,

How is it going with tadpole? I hope you are keeping good care of him or her. I'm a bit worried about my own baby, to be honest. Robyn's looking a little peaky, and after years of trying to get her to do schoolwork, now that's all she does. She even said that maybe she'd outgrown the marvelous Martin the other day. Said she couldn't see the point of him coming around anymore. "Well," I told her, "he's the person I hold responsible for all your recent flourishing." Then she ran out of the room, banging the door behind her. I know it's just a teenage thing because I remember us doing it. Or me, anyway. You and Mum didn't really argue, did you? I used to be so jealous of that. I know she could be a pain, always wanting to know what we were up to, but I miss it now. I wish someone would just ask me sometimes what I thought I was doing and get cross with me like she used to. Because they cared.

Nell

123. NOTE FROM GEORGE GRIFFITHS TO
BRENDA LEWIS (ATTACHED TO 124)

Dear Brenda,

Please find enclosed the first minutes of The Pilgrim House Residents Committee.

Yours sincerely,
George Griffiths,
Chair

124. MINUTES OF THE
PILGRIM RESIDENTS COMMITTEE

Present George Griffiths (GG)
Martin Morris (MM)
Florence Oliver (FO)

Apologies Annabel Armstrong (in absentia)

1. **Minutes of previous meeting.**
   This is normally when the minutes of the last meeting held would be read out and approved, but because this is the first one, GG discussed protocol at length and told us that this is something we should do in the future.

2. **Thefts.**
   GG stated that although the robberies at Pilgrim House had abated lately, it was still something that should be kept an eye on. Both MM and FO said they thought it might just have been a phase. GG said they should try to have it happen to them and see how they feel.

3. **Use of tea and coffee.**
   GG said he was disappointed that residents hadn't been

filling in the chart he had prepared for tea and coffee usage. FO said she wasn't sure she was tall enough to reach it, and MM said there wasn't often a pen in the kitchen and he wasn't going to go looking for one when all he wanted was a quick cuppa. GG is going to fix a pen to the chart by means of tape and string. FO said she liked having Keith Crosbie around the place, and MM said he bet she did. GG called the meeting to order.

4. **Talks.**

FO said she thought Nell Baker had done us all proud with her entertaining and enjoyable talk. GG admitted he'd found it very emotional, and MM said he wondered about getting someone in to talk about poetry. After discussion, it was agreed that MM would ask Robyn to come and speak. GG said he would have liked to ask Robyn himself, but he agreed that it might be more professional coming from a nonfamily member. FO said it would be lovely to have young people around the place more and wondered about asking Sophi to talk about university. GG said that maybe she could learn to spell her name properly first.

5. **Staff hygiene.**

After GG said he thought it wasn't appropriate for staff to have defiled hands, there was considerable discussion. FO said she thought every bit of Steve was just perfect, and MM reported that tattoos on hands were a sign of a prison stay. FO said in which case bygones should be left as bygones, but GG said he was deeply worried about the impact the knowledge of this might have on certain residents and would be writing to Brenda for confirmation that police checks on all staff were carried out. FO said he was stuffy, and the meeting ended.

Additional note from GG: Although some alterations to language in these minutes have been made, after considerable discussion it was agreed to leave them as FO's account of events, and they will be commented on at the next meeting. However, it is important to point out that the well-being of residents such as Catherine Francis, who might not have seen so much life as others, is of paramount importance. It should also be noted that in the future committee members are not expected to leave the meeting until the Chair has called it officially to a close.

This is FO writing this: The above was added without my agreement. And there is nothing wrong with plain language that everybody can easily understand. However, the "considerable discussion" this "engendered" was not "considered paramount" when GG rewrote much of what I wrote. If people are going to be given jobs, they should be allowed to get on with them. That is FO's view, anyway. And there's no point in stuffiness just for the sake of it.

125. LETTER FROM MARTIN MORRIS TO MO GRIFFITHS

Dear Mo,

I had forgotten how good it feels to be behind a camera. It's the power it gives you. Not the useless everyday power of being able to say "stand over there" or "smile," but the more important power of being anonymous. Although I take the picture, it's not me who has the responsibility for what happens after. That's all down to the viewer. Viewer, voyeur. The similarity isn't a coincidence. Well, not in my photographs anyway. That's why I always get the models to look at the lens so the viewer has to admit they're staring at a human being, not just a breast, or a body, or a dream. There's always more there than a fragment, or even a series of fragments.

You see, when I was photographing Florence, I was thinking about you. Because I've been snatching at too many different fragments of you recently and I would give everything to have you look back at me. Or to be able to see you properly, and not through Nell's or Robyn's eyes. And especially not through George's eyes.

Take the other day. I asked George about your hair. It's not as daft as it sounds because I've got him to arrange a hair appointment for Nell. It was all part of my original plan to get Angie back, you see. I figured if he started making a fuss over Nell, then Angie would get jealous and come home.

"Did you ever make an appointment for your Maureen?" I asked him. We were sitting on our bench. The one around which I spread your cornflower seeds. I like to talk to him there, thinking about how you'll soon be springing up to join us.

Anyway, he looked at me as if I'd belched. "No, no, no," he said. I'm not joking. He really did three no's in a row like that. "She did all that kind of thing herself. Much more suitable." And he did that bark he does. The one where he shuts his eyes.

Suitable? What could be more suitable than beautifying the woman you love?

"And she kept her hair long, did she?" I asked. I knew you hadn't because I'd seen you just after it was cut the first time. You kept putting your hand up to your neck and feeling the bare space. I didn't like it to begin with, but I got used to it. Just took a bit longer than it would have done if you'd have been with me every day. But what I wanted to know was what made you cut your hair. Your beautiful hair.

"I don't think she ever had what you might call long hair," he said then. "Or at least not after the children were born. Maureen was never one for thinking about her looks. She preferred to be practical."

Well, I wanted to say, the Mo I knew cared about how she looked right enough, but I bit my tongue. It's a wonder there's any left these days.

But then I realized a haircut wasn't going to be enough to get this girl of ours back home where she belongs. Somehow, if she's like you, I think it will take more than just a bit of jealousy. So I have been hatching a better plan to bring her back. Something that she won't be able to say no to.

And when she's here, I can get her. She will be the final piece of the jigsaw that brings all our fragments together.

"Do you believe in infinity, George?" I asked him. He doesn't like a question without a factual yes or no answer, but I wanted to know what he thought. Because the hope that you and I will be together in the end is the only thing that keeps me going and I needed to hear it from him.

"Not now, Martin," he said, as if I were a child. He wanted to get back to talking about Nell, and whether I thought she'd think less of him, worrying about a woman's haircut.

But I do. I believe in infinity. I just wish it would come sooner.

M

126. NOTE FROM ROBYN BAKER TO MARTIN MORRIS

Dear Martin,

You know I can't come in and do a poetry reading to the Pilgrims, and especially not when you've got my other poems and stories still. Please don't do this to me.

Robyn

127. NOTE FROM BRENDA LEWIS TO
STEVE JENKINS (ATTACHED TO 124)

Here are George's committee notes I was telling you about. Is there nothing you can do to head this off before it goes any further? Maybe take George to the pub or find something else that will use up his energy. Helen Elliott came to see me this afternoon, annoyed at not being included. She thought I'd set it up and it was official. I have a bad feeling about this. I suppose if the worse comes to the worst, we could always say we couldn't read the handwriting.

Bren

128. NOTE FROM FLORENCE OLIVER TO LIZZIE CORN

Dear Lizzie,

It was good to catch up on all your news in your last letter. What a lot has been going on. I think it's very positive of Laurie to take that attitude about Amy's teacher calling her in to talk about Troy because there are many mothers who might be devastated. Still, as you are always telling me, mothers know best. And if Laurie isn't worried about Amy taking up massaging, then I wouldn't worry at all if I were you.

Now Lizzie, I would like to tell you about the photography session because I know you and how you will have been thinking the worst. It wasn't at all what I expected. I walked up and down the corridor outside Martin's room a fair few times before knocking on his door, I can tell you. But then, I did that thing you taught me of locking my knees together and deep breathing, and I walked straight in.

I'd been planning all the things I was going to say. I'd even made a note of jokes I could make, but Martin didn't even turn around, so I just stood there. He'd got his camera hung around his neck and he was fiddling with the lens. I coughed, and he still didn't look up. Just nodded his head toward where I could see he'd got a chair from the kitchen and placed it in the middle of the room. There was a sheet draped over the back. Also, something I couldn't work out at first, but then I got it. One of Brenda's aprons. And a dish towel and a mixing bowl from the kitchen. My first thought was how he'd catch it when Matron found him stealing all these things, but my second was about where I was going to get undressed. IF I did. Third, I wasn't sure I wanted to get dressed up as a cook. I'd been expecting something glam. Not cooking.

And that's when I knew I couldn't do it. "You can take a picture of me," I said, "but you'll not get me to take my clothes off."

He looked up then, almost startled.

"Florence," he said, as if he had to remind himself who I was, although, as you know, he normally calls me Mrs. Oliver.

I could feel my hands clench into fists at my side.

"Go on then," I said. "If you're going to take it, make it quick. If you really do have film in your camera, that is."

He went even more ghostlike than usual. It was the first time I'd been in his room. It's so small that it's hard for him to take a step back, but he did. Although his shoulders brushed the wall, he didn't seem to notice.

"Stay right there," he said. "Don't move."

So I just kept on standing there. When I let my hands relax, he said no. I was to clench them again and I was to look at him, just as I'd been doing before. Like I didn't really like him very much. That gave me a shock, because it was as if he was mind reading. I didn't like him much at that moment. I was full of angry feelings. So I glared at him. I thought if he was Graham standing in front of me now, this is how I'd be staring at him. Like an insect I could just tread on. He wouldn't know what had hit him because I'd never let him treat me now like he used to.

And through all this, Martin snip-snapped away. Once he told me to look over his shoulder, another time down at the ground, but mostly I just looked straight into the lens. I didn't exactly forget it was Martin on the other side, but I stopped caring. He kept up this chatter about how well I was doing, how good the photographs would be, although when he put the camera down and said that was enough, I didn't want to stop. I wanted just to keep standing there, glowering.

"Is that it?" I asked. My fingers were aching from how I'd been clenching them so I flexed them a bit. I didn't know what I wanted him to say. Except it wasn't just that I was beautiful anymore. No, I wanted him to say I was powerful, an Amazon, someone who mattered. All Woman. Do you know, Lizzie, I do believe if he'd have asked me, I could have even roared right then.

"Do you always want more?" he asked. And he did that arching eyebrow thing that made me laugh and it broke the moment, which was a relief really. I thought about how he'd called me a minx right at the beginning and what a shock it had given me. So he put the camera up and took another photo of me laughing, and then he said if I wanted I could undo a few buttons on my dress, and I thought, well, yes, maybe I could. First off, I just showed one shoulder, pulling my bra strap down and I took the pins out of my hair. He took a photograph of me like that.

"I bet you've got a beautiful back," he said then. And I thought no one in my life has ever commented on my back. I wasn't sure anyone had even looked at it. So I turned around and let my dress slip down so he could see it. My heart was beating because I was facing the door, and I prayed no one would come in because what on earth would they think we were up to.

"Will you let me?" Martin said, and I didn't know what he was asking at first, but then I realized he wanted me to undo my bra strap. I nodded. I wanted to cry, and I knew I would if I looked around. But he did it ever so gently. He only fumbled a little bit.

Graham never bothered to undo it, you know. He'd only pull it up, but Martin obviously knew what he was doing. I still didn't take my bra off completely, or my dress, although I thought if he touched my skin, I might pop.

"Beautiful," Martin said. I heard him move away, so I straightened up and let the dress fall down a little bit more, although not below my waist. I heard the camera click.

"Florence," Martin called. "Will you look over your shoulder at me? Make me the happiest man alive."

So I tried, but my rheumatism was playing up and, besides, I felt all shy, as if we were waking up in bed together, like the first morning with Graham on our honeymoon. When I still loved him. Before I was frightened of him. And it became all mixed up. It was so sweet, so tender in Martin's room, just as it had been in that B&B with Graham that I forgot what a stupid old fool I was. And how someone like your Troy would laugh at me if he saw what we were doing. It was just me and Martin together. And do you know, at that moment, I was one of them at last, Lizzie. I was one of them proper women I used to look at in Graham's magazines.

I went back to my room after we'd finished, and just lay on my bed until supper time. I'd been so many different sorts of women in Martin's room. All the Florences I had no idea were hidden inside of me had come out to have a gander. It was strange, Lizzie, because that's exactly what it felt like, as if it was me who was doing the looking, not Martin. And yet, he was taking the pictures of me, wasn't he?

I didn't even feel ashamed of having taken my dress half off in front of a man who wasn't my husband. Or a doctor. If anything, it was the first shots when I'd been fully dressed and staring that disturbed me the most. Because that was the real me. And when he saw me, he didn't turn away, Lizzie. Not even a little bit.

Am I making any sense? I'm not even sure what happened in Martin's room myself. But I do know I've been clutching your little white handkerchief so hard since, it's a wonder it's still in one piece. And here is another funny thing. After we'd finished, Martin said something to me that I didn't take in at the time. It was only when I was back in my room that I realized how he'd said how lucky I was being born a woman.

I suppose we have to wait now for the photographs to come, but I don't know if I even want to see them. It was enough to have them taken.

Anyway, enough of silly old me. Flirty Flo, you'll be saying. Let me know about the school, won't you, and although we haven't always seen eye to eye, wish Laurie well. However brave she's being, it must be difficult. She's lucky to have you.

Yours aye,

Flo

129. EMAIL FROM NELL BAKER TO ANGIE GRIFFITHS

Hello Angie,

It's your newly shorn sister here. So I finally had my appointment with Dad's hairdresser, and even if I say it myself, it's not too bad. Even Robyn has given it the seal of approval. You would have laughed at Dad. He only waited outside with Martin while I was being done. They set up these chairs outside the room, and the two of them sat there until I was finished. Mrs. Oliver came too. The three of them have formed quite a little clique. Can you imagine Dad with friends? I can't tell you the relief of not having him on my back the whole time, but I do wonder what Mum would have made of it. Don't tell me you never imagined what it would have been like to have had a normal family because I know you used to lie at school, too, and pretend we had people around on Sundays and stuff because I looked in your books. I don't think I ever told you how I wrote an essay once about how we'd been on holiday with another family. It was full of lies. "Every evening we ate and played together," as if that was something marvelous. But then the teacher put it up on the wall, so before parents' night I had to find a way of creeping into the classroom and tearing it down so Mum wouldn't see it. I never knew whether Mrs. Clifford had mentioned it to her.

But now Dad has more of a social life than me. They've even set up a committee which will apparently suit him just fine. "Have you got a file?" I asked him as a joke. You know what he had always been like with his files, but apparently Mrs. Oliver has bested him here. She's the committee secretary and has got TWO files. If she wasn't so keen on Martin, I might say she and Dad could get together and open their own filing cabinet. It's a thought.

Will try to attach a photograph of the hair anyway. I need your opinion before I hit the streets of Bedford with confidence. Mark says it's OK, but he would. He's always hanging around me at work now wanting to talk about cooking. I tease him that it's food porn.

Nell

130. ANSWER PHONE MESSAGE FROM
GEORGE GRIFFITHS TO ANGIE GRIFFITHS

Hello Angie,

This is your father speaking to you. Or speaking to your machine. Thank you for your card of a French apple tart with your note on the back about your mother's cooking. I wanted to tell you that we always knew it was you who ate that whole date and walnut loaf one day after school. She couldn't stop laughing when she told me, but we pretended we thought someone might have crept into the house to steal it to see if you would own up. Even when Nell had nightmares about the phantom cake thief, you still said nothing. You always were such a stubborn child. And so hungry. Mind you, poor Nell was always having nightmares. If it wasn't a cake thief, it was a playground spy or a Christmas-tree robber.

We even had to get rid of the big trees we used to have every year because of that last one.

At least I was able to do something nice for her the other day. She had her hair cut by one of the girls who comes here, and I must say she looks beautiful. I can't claim all the credit because it was Martin's idea. He thought Nell needed cheering up, but that she'd prefer the idea to come from me. I will never get to grips with the fairer sex, but it seems to have done the trick.

Martin said that one of the helpers here, Steve, thought she looked the cat's meow, not that this is anything to boast about. Steve isn't really quite the thing. I'm not sure why Mrs. Oliver and Martin give him the time of day. I am trying to get his police records at the moment. Do you have contacts? I had hopes for Nell with a policeman she seemed to be friendly with, but Martin tells me I was mistaken.

Anyway, if you want your hair cut, I will be pleased to arrange it. I think even you with your Parisian standards would be satisfied with young Chrissie's work.

Angie, I forgot to say it is six minutes past two on Thursday afternoon and this has been your father.

131. EMAIL FROM NELL BAKER TO ANGIE GRIFFITHS

Dad said I looked beautiful??? Holy moly.

132. NOTE FROM CLAUDE BICHOURIE TO
ANGIE GRIFFITHS

Angela,

I cannot understand your note at all, or why you are angry with me. Am I not always telling you how beautiful you are? And what do you mean you had some photographs taken? But this is a good thing, no? Particularly if I am understanding rightly what you mean by a sweetheart shot. You are a wicked beautiful girl, and I am the luckiest man in Paris.

I will be with you tomorrow night.

133. EMAIL FROM NELL BAKER TO ANGIE GRIFFITHS

No, I don't remember Mum ever having photographs taken at all. It doesn't sound exactly like the kind of thing she would do, does it? I seem to remember she hated posing for the camera more than anything.

But here's a strange thing. After I read your email, I went to look at the few photographs we've got of Mum and one of them has gone. I can't find it anywhere.

I suppose Robyn might have got it. After James left us, I found this box full of photographs of him at the back of a cupboard. Not whole photographs, but bits of his face she'd cut out of other pictures. I didn't say anything because I thought she'd grow out of it. I'll ask her when she comes back but she's very sensitive at the moment. She burst out crying yesterday just because I said there was an old woman outside work trying to get across the road and the cars wouldn't stop for her. I felt awful.

Why don't you just ask Dad whether Mum ever went to a photographer? He's changed a lot recently. He's almost normal.

Kiss to tadpole. Will you tell Dad about him or her too? It's killing me keeping it a secret.

134. LETTER FROM MARTIN MORRIS TO ROBYN BAKER

Dear Robyn,

Your very dramatic letter touched me tremendously. Please don't worry any longer about me coming to your house for our reading sessions, enjoyable as they have been. I will write to your mother immediately and tell her how the kind of thing you are writing has been too much for me. She will be puzzled but will soon understand what I mean when I show her your work.

Also put your little mind at rest regarding the poetry reading here. It is hard to stand up in public and say your own words at the best of times. So I will save you the trouble. How about if I read them out myself? You won't need to be there, but I will make sure you get all of the glory.

However shy they may claim to be, there is nothing worse for an artist than not to get the recognition they deserve. Trust me on that one. I don't intend for that to happen to you. What a pity you don't have your father to protect you. I imagine that he would have known what to do in a situation like this.

Yours,
Martin

135. EMAIL FROM NELL BAKER TO ANGIE GRIFFITHS

There's something wrong with Robyn. I'm worried sick. It's not just her being a teenager anymore, but when she looks at me her eyes seem dead and I can't get her to talk at all. I hate to say it, Angie, but it reminds me of when you and Mum weren't getting on at the end. That's why I'm writing now. Tell me what would have helped. Please, Angie, tell me what I'm doing wrong and how I can make things better.

136. LETTER FROM FLORENCE OLIVER TO LIZZIE CORN

Dear Lizzie,

Does Laurie have any actual grounds for suspecting you of being the one who went to the school about Troy? She must at least let you tell your side of the story so you can prove her wrong.

Unless.

Lizzie, you didn't, did you?

Oh love. I hoped you would have learned your lesson after what happened when you told Graham about me and the butcher becoming friends in Aldershot. Just because you are right *in fact* doesn't always mean you are right *in truth*. If you know what I mean.

But I'm not going to jump to conclusions. I will wait for you to tell me the truth. And I feel for you having Troy's mother to stay because I can imagine it must be getting very crowded in Laurie's house. It must be confusing for Brian and Amy to have two grannies, but you are blood so you will always have their hearts. Even despite Cora's homemade puddings and the card games and the fact that Laurie's not speaking to you at the moment because of the tale telling. I don't know any good card games myself, but I will ask Susan Reed. She always seems to be happily busy with grandchildren, so she might have some ideas for me to pass on.

How about bingo? Just a thought. We did love it when we played it despite the fighting after. Shall we give it another whirl in Bournemouth?

And the answer to your question is no. I still haven't seen the photographs. I'm not sure I even want to. Just having them taken is a secret I keep hugging tight to myself.

Yours aye,

Flo

137. LETTER FROM MARTIN MORRIS TO MO GRIFFITHS

Dear Mo,

So our girl still isn't coming back.

As I suspected, the haircut wasn't enough. According to George, Angie has even seen a photograph of Nell and approves. But she's too busy to come home. "Oooh," he says, rubbing his hands together as if all the money she makes is going direct to his bank account. "She's got such a big job." The funny thing is that Nell calls it the same thing, but no one says exactly what this "big job" is.

No, the situation has called for something else, something more dramatic. A family crisis, I thought. And who is the one who is most likely to cause a crisis? The one they all look to for trouble? Robyn, of course. There is always one in a family who carries the burden of all wrong-doing. Plus I know Robyn will do anything to stop her mother getting upset. Even things against her better judgment. She's playing right into my hands, although I have to say she's still proving rather slow.

I can't feel bad because these are desperate times. And, all things being equal, I think your family owes me one. Besides, once Angie's back, everything will be much better.

And just so Nell doesn't feel completely forgotten, I have a plan for her too.

M

138. ANSWER PHONE FROM
GEORGE GRIFFITHS TO ANGIE GRIFFITHS

This is your father here. At his wit's end. Your father's ends. Normally nothing gives me more satisfaction than being proven right, but this time, I find no comfort in it.

Do you remember how, some time ago, I told you about how I suspected young Robyn of creeping into my room and taking things? At that time, I dropped a few heavy hints and the thieving stopped, but now it seems I was wrong to let sleeping dogs lie. I blame myself for taking my eye off the ball. Robyn, not content with robbing her own family, has been caught stealing from one of our dear friends, Martin Morris, who I have learned has put himself out considerably on her behalf.

Nell is beside herself, which is of no help as the girl clearly needs professional support. I am advising Nell to get the police involved to teach her a lesson. It seems harsh but it is time for action.

We are lucky that Martin is being so understanding about it all, but nevertheless, this is a family matter and, although he is adamant that he does not want to press charges, I do believe we have to make amends somehow.

Thank you for your postcard of French breads. I wonder why they need so many shapes. Very unnecessary in my view.

Your father

139. EMAIL FROM NELL BAKER TO ANGIE GRIFFITHS

Yep, this time Dad has got it right. Bloody Robyn. She's upstairs in her room sobbing her heart out, and I can't get any sense out of her at all. I'll email more later. And to think she did it to Martin of all people. He reckons she was after one of his cameras. I'm going to get her to apologize. It's the least she can do.

140. NOTE FROM CLAUDE BICHOURIE TO ANGELA GRIFFITHS

Chérie,

Why on earth do you need to go to England now? Is it because of the photographs? Or because I haven't been attentive enough recently. I have been at a loss to understand you recently, but the truth is I have started to think about you more than I should. My office will send you first-class air tickets to travel to London in six weeks' time. Your visit will then coincide when I will be away in the country. Until then, I crave your company all for myself.

Claude

141. LETTER FROM MARTIN MORRIS TO NELL BAKER

Dear Nell,

It was kind of you to write but there is really no need. Although my initial reaction at finding Robyn rummaging through my room was one of shock, I wonder now if I overreacted by mentioning it to anyone. As I have told George, we were all young once, and the last thing I would like to do is to cause problems for your family, particularly when you have been so kind to a lonely old man.

If it would make you feel better to encourage Robyn to write a letter of apology, then I would be happy to accept it, but once again, there is no obligation.

Nothing would make me happier than for Robyn and me to put all this fuss behind us and be good friends again. Even so, I'm sure you understand why my little visits to your home must come to an end, much as they have come to mean the world to me. In the meantime, if I own anything at all she would like, even my best camera, then all she has to do is ask for it. I still think she is a wonderful girl and I hope that you will tell her this.

Yours sincerely,
Martin

142. LETTER FROM MARTIN MORRIS TO MO GRIFFITHS

Dear Mo,

Personally I thought my letter to Nell was a little too much, but I hear it's done the trick. Angie is coming home. George has just let slip that she will be here in six weeks' time. I'd prefer tomorrow, but at least she's on her way.

Poor Robyn has written me a letter of apology. Under duress, of course, but I'm being magnanimous. I would feel sorry for her if I wasn't convinced these are all useful lessons she is learning. I don't think she will make the same mistake of being so trusting ever again, and I am sure in time she will be grateful to me.

My only sadness is that Marta must have lied about me because the boys next door say they are not allowed to talk to me anymore because I am apparently "creepy." Marta's replacement has taken to glowering at me and ushering them inside every time I go out to the yard. She is a hefty Swede, all blond hair and teeth. Now, there is no crying at night, and it feels lonely all over again up on my top floor.

M

143. ANSWER PHONE MESSAGE FROM
GEORGE GRIFFITHS TO ANGIE GRIFFITHS

Angie, this is George Griffiths, your father.

Your sister has told me of your plans finally to visit us and I am very pleased. Let's hope that this time no last-minute work meetings occur. I only wish the circumstances could be happier.

Thanks to Martin's intervention and levelheadedness, and because none of us can get to the bottom of what she wanted from Martin's room, we have agreed to try to forget Robyn's lapse.

I am not convinced this is the right way forward, but if there is any good side to this situation, it is that I have managed to persuade Nell that the girl needs to see her father. It appears that Martin has been giving her private coaching. They did not want to tell me until Robyn had learned some of the poems your mother loved so much, although I will confide in you that I am perplexed that they would think this would be something I might enjoy. Although you girls have laughed at me for it, haven't I always said that no good will come from poetry? It is not the stuff of everyday life.

I hope you will not mind me saying that I wish you were coming here sooner. To dress a cat up in a black beret and striped T-shirt and sell it as a postcard seems typically French and very unnatural to me. I am disturbed that you might think it funny and am starting to wonder if you have been teasing me with all your cards. In which case, I will try to see the joke. Perhaps a sense of humor is a valuable asset in these difficult times.

Your father

144. LETTER FROM FLORENCE OLIVER TO LIZZIE CORN

Dear Lizzie,

I know I am getting out of turn with our letter writing but I need your urgent counsel, pet. You see, last week Martin found Robyn in his room. He was worried in case Robyn had found his stack of photographs, and concerned she might not understand properly what they were, what with her being so young.

So he told George, who of course hit the roof. Not about the photographs. In fact, it turns out he is quite the connoisseur of those, fancy, but it seems he already had suspicions that Robyn had been stealing from HIS room, so he put two and two together and made five. But the thing is, Lizzie, I know—and you know—that it was ME taking things from George's room, not poor Robyn.

So what am I to do? Do I say something, and risk all those hours I've spent talking investments with George, or do I let Robyn stew?

Martin says he has no hard feelings against Robyn, but of course he doesn't know about me either. Mind, George keeps going on about some seeds, and I know I never took those. But what would a teenage girl want with gardening?

It has hit Nell hard. Well, I suppose it would what with that man she was so keen on being a policeman. Martin says we should concentrate on her, and maybe find her a new boyfriend, he says. Apparently I got it wrong about the policeman.

"Us?" I asked him. "Where are we going to find someone Nell's age?"

But then who should walk into the room but Steve Jenkins. He's been a little down since Sophi left. "Are you thinking what I'm thinking?" I nudged Martin, but he shook his head.

"George really wouldn't like it," he said.

"Nell might," I said, "because he's a sight for sore eyes, is Steve. Got plans too, you can tell. He needs a mature woman." I nudged him again, but somehow my elbow must have hit his rib in the wrong way because he yelped, and Steve came running over to see what the trouble was, and obviously we couldn't carry on our little conversation then.

And now as I write this letter, I don't think I am going to mention stealing from his room to George. What's in the past is in the past, and what good will raking over it again bring? Besides, we need to be looking forward to the future. Now Sophi has gone back to college, I imagine Steve is a bit lonely. Imagine if we had a wedding. Wouldn't that be lovely?

Any news on that front from Troy and Laurie, by the way? It might just be the answer to your problems. I should think little Amy would love to be a bridesmaid and it would be a way of making Laurie appreciate you more. All girls need their mothers at weddings, even if it is their third trot up the aisle.

I do hope she will be a bit more friendly toward you soon.

Yours aye,

Flo

145. EMAIL FROM NELL BAKER TO ANGIE GRIFFITHS

I called James last night and said we had to work this out together. That if we weren't careful, Robyn would go completely to the bad. He did that *now, now,* tutting thing he does, so I told him to shut up. And that I was bringing Robyn to him the next weekend and like it or not the two of them were going to learn to have some kind of relationship. Dad's right. We've let Robyn have her own way for far too long.

I should have done this years ago. The strange thing is that Robyn seems relieved too. And at work, Mark caught me smiling. "More flowers?" he said, so I told him what had happened, and he said if I was free over the weekend, maybe I'd like to go walking with him. I would. It feels as if I haven't done anything apart from work, look after Robyn, or listen to Dad moan for years.

And OK, he's not exactly the corporate giant Dad always planned for me, or even an architect like James, but he makes me laugh. Besides, who else am I going to find in Bedfordshire?

So you're really coming this time, are you? I must say I'm surprised that Mr. Married Frog is letting you off the leash for a bit. Especially now. He does know about the baby, doesn't he? I suppose the French do these things differently.

146. LETTER FROM MARTIN MORRIS TO MO GRIFFITHS

Dear Mo,

Knowing I am going to meet Angie at last made me nervous. At breakfast my cup just slipped out of my hands and crashed down to the floor. My trousers were covered in tea, Susan Reed shouted, and Steve came fussing around with a dishcloth.

"Good job you're not Brenda or I would be arresting you for feeling me up." I tried to make a joke of it, but no one else smiled so I stopped. I was feeling a bit shaky, to be honest. And grateful the tea was only lukewarm.

"Martin, are you all right?" Mrs. Oliver kept fussing, and even Keith Crosbie came blinking in from his books to see what the commotion was all about.

Do you think Angie and I will get on? I can't ask Robyn because it seems she and I aren't talking at the moment. Everybody else has agreed to put her little forage in my room behind them, but apparently she's finding it difficult. George even told me he thought it better for everyone if she didn't come to Pilgrim House for a bit. Better for who? Not me, that's for sure, now her little escapade has done the trick.

I wish my hands would stop shaking. I'm going into town this afternoon to pick up the photographs I took of Mrs. Oliver. Time was when I would have walked all the way to the shops, enjoyed looking into the windows of all the houses I passed and seeing the lives on show, but I'm too tired these days. Even an afternoon listening to your husband nattering on makes me sleepy. We need some jollying up here. Perhaps this plan to pair Nell up with Steve will keep us busy until Angie arrives.

M

147. LETTER FROM FLORENCE OLIVER TO LIZZIE CORN

Dear Lizzie,

Rejoice! Hang out the flags. Let me do a jig for you.

Annabel has come back to us.

There we all were sitting around dozing in the afternoon,

when she walked into the room just as if she'd never been away. She even did her little curtsey bob, so it wasn't like when Elizabeth Rogers came back that time and she was statue-like from the pills. No, Annabel took her seat, folded down her dress over her knees in that little-girl way of hers, and beamed around at us.

Helen and Catherine were with me. "Annabel," Helen said, with not a touch of mischief in her voice for once, "it's good to see you." And it was. I wanted to rush over to the other side of the room and kiss her. She was like a blessing showing us we could cheat the other side a little too. The four of us just smiled at each other. Little Annabel. Who would have thought she'd be the one to beat them all.

So now we are back to a full house and life feels a bit more settled. It's just what we need after the upset we had with Robyn. Martin says our job is to keep George busy, and he says I'm a genius with my idea of organizing a committee to get Nell together with Steve, but the thing is, Lizzie, I can't remember suggesting this exactly. I've been a bit worried I'm going a bit forgetful. Perhaps I did take the seeds from George's room? I still feel bad about not saying anything about Robyn, although Martin blames himself. He says he might have taken being a father figure to the girl too far. I might ask Martin what he thinks about her joining our little committee. It would be a way of getting her back on good terms with everyone.

I'm sorry Troy got so het up about the bingo. Is bingo gambling? Just a bit of fun I would have thought, and you weren't to know that Brian would force Amy to give him her pocket money for winning.

The other thing I'm thinking of, Lizzie, have you still got Frank's ceremonial knife? The kiddies would love that, especially if you told them a few of the stories Graham and Frank told us about their fighting days. Remember how they used to make us scream! It would make them respect their granddaddy, and Laurie did love her daddy so much, didn't she? I seethed inside myself when I read that Cora had asked Laurie to call her Mum. As if she didn't have the best mother already. She is just a step.

Still, you and I, pet, we've battled with worse, and at least we're thinking now of how to get our own back. I think it was the photo session that did it for me. I don't want to put that feisty girl I was in front of the camera away now.

Yours aye,
Flo

148. NOTE FROM FLORENCE OLIVER TO MARTIN MORRIS

I have been thinking that if you ever wanted another photographic session, then I wouldn't mind. Just you and me. Apart from that, we are having a little celebration tonight for Annabel coming home. Six o'clock in the sitting room.

149. LETTER FROM MARTIN MORRIS TO ROBYN BAKER

Dear Robyn,

Thank you for your letter of apology, which I am happy to accept in the spirit with which it was written. I am very glad we will have the chance to be friends again, and I wondered if you would like to come to Pilgrim House next Thursday after school for tea with me, your grandfather, and Mrs. Oliver. It will be a chance to show we have put unpleasant things behind us.

With best wishes as always,
Martin

150. LETTER FROM MARTIN MORRIS TO MO GRIFFITHS

Dear Mo,

Everyone is always going on here about how good-looking this Steve Jenkins is, but I have never seen the appeal of the male body. There's a beauty in a woman's shape, a lack if you like, that makes the lines just soft enough for photographs. You can capture the way the light and the dark plays on the skin. It's not about exposing the body, nothing to do with just taking off clothes and snapping away. No, it's about creating a dream. One in which you can almost taste the desire of both parties, although I can't believe that women would ever really desire in the same way a man does. It's always seemed to me that what a woman likes most is for a man to take control of the loving. A woman needs to be cared for, and a man needs to do that caring. A woman to be looked at, a man to look.

Call me old-fashioned if you like, but I always knew you liked me watching you. There would be times when I'd be standing outside your house, and I'd catch sight of your shadow behind the net curtains you put up, and I'd know you were moving just for me. I hated those curtains at first, thought you were shutting me out, but then I realized that, if I looked very hard, I could see you better. It would be just as it was in my best photographs. My customers never actually saw the breasts, the triangle between the legs, but they knew what was there and they knew that if they took one step further, if they crossed the line, all of the woman could be theirs. It was important to leave it as their decision.

That's what it felt you were doing to me. I could have crossed the line, walked up your path and rang your doorbell, but somehow there was always tomorrow. And then I'd be there again the next day, watching, and I'd see a bit more. And so it went on. I could shut out the others, see, from where I was standing in the street. I could make out your silhouette, but not George's, or Nell's, or even Angie's. So I saw what I liked.

But here, it's as if I'm pulling back the curtains. I have been coloring in the outlines for George and Nell, and now I'm about to step through the window and take Angie. There's still work to be done, but nothing can stop me now. Even so, I can't help but wonder what I'll be losing.

You see, I got back the photographs of Florence Oliver today, and they showed me again some of the magic of keeping to the other side of the net curtain. I could tell when I went to pick them up that they'd been looking at them. The boy serving me had the pimply neck of someone who still hasn't grown up properly. "Ah," he said a bit too loudly when I gave my name. "Mr. Morris, eh?" And a girl peered out from the doorway at the back. It must have been a prearranged signal, I suppose. They wanted to have a laugh. Well let them, I thought. They're young. They probably wondered whether to call the police when they first saw the photographs. Was there a rule with old folk and nudity, they might have thought, in the same way there was with kids? Was it decent? Proper? Surely there were laws against it.

I waited until I was back in my room before I opened the packet. Just as I suspected, the photographs had been flicked through. Probably a few times. You could tell by the way they'd lost their stickiness. I thought Florence might like that, because what was the point in having your photograph taken if no one was going to see it. Besides, I doubted they would recognize her next time she shuffled up to the counter, even in that new bright red coat of hers. I'd done it again. I still had it in me to create the dream.

I forgot for a moment that the photographs were to trick, and I wanted to yell with happiness. You should see the look she gave in the one with her bare back. I forgot all about the sagging skin, the veins, the blemishes that seem to bloom on old skin. Instead, I saw the kindness on offer, Mo. And a little bit of a challenge. That's what I love most about women. The way everything gets so mixed up in you.

I won't show them to her just yet. She's after more already, but what she wants is that time in front of the camera. She wants to be looked at, see.

And it seems I'm the only one left to do the looking for her.

M

151. LETTER FROM FLORENCE OLIVER TO LIZZIE CORN

Dear Lizzie,

This fretting will be no good for you. Calm yourself down.

Remember the time James Barton's wife tried to take over the Young Wives of NCOs Club? How we let her think she was part of us first, and it was only when she relaxed her guard that we showed her that we knew exactly what we were doing. The final straw was when we put her in charge of the rummage sale, and she had her shoulder wrenched opening the doors because none of us told her she had to organize the crowd outside in an orderly line.

By the time she came back from the emergency room, she was prepared to admit that her ideas weren't better, just different, and she started the Arts and Film Club, which never proved popular enough to be dangerous. It was the same time as we began our letter-writing campaign to the soldiers who didn't have anyone to write to. Admittedly that didn't last long, not with them writing back to ask if we'd send them nude photographs and Graham finding out. But it proved we could come up with new ideas too.

But I'm deviating here, although remind me to come back to the photographs. So Cornelia Barton kept friendly with us after, but she also knew we had won. You see why I'm telling you this. It's because of Cora. You need to show her that you're not frightened of her. That the time she's spending with Brian and Amy isn't better than anything you might do, even if it involves slightly less money.

I'm glad the shopping went well. I didn't even know they did bras for children as young as Amy, but if it made her happy, then that's what is important. And yes, I can imagine how excited they were when you took them to the café and said they could have anything to eat they wanted. Funny for Brian to choose an oatmeal cookie, but I bet Amy loved her bun and I imagine you did have a giggle together about them looking like boob cakes with those cherries on top!

And to think three months ago we had little to get excited about, Lizzie. What with all the things that have happened to us recently, it's a wonder we're still standing. What did that Chinese man say, may you live in interesting times. He's supposed to have meant it as a curse, but all I can say is that he didn't live in boring old Pilgrim House before Martin came.

Even George has a spring in his step these days, and the other day he went to his room and got Keith the big dictionary. He'd been hiding it because it is only supposed to be used by residents. Helen and Catherine have taken to going to a book club at the library every month as well as their regular Friday jaunts, and are talking about joining a garden visiting club over the summer. You and I will have to get on with planning our holiday or we will be quite left behind.

Even Annabel has taken to waiting on the steps for the milkman, and begging him to teach her new songs. Admittedly, she will scare us half to death by suddenly bellowing in our ears about virgins and sailors when we're not expecting it, but the new washer-dryer her son has just donated to Pilgrim House is, according to Steve, a dream, so I think we'll have to put up with

Annabel's singing for a little while longer. Willingly too, I say, when you consider the alternative.

And now there was something else I meant to tell you, but I have forgotten. You take care, pet. Remember Cornelia Barton and how all it took for her to be defeated was a herd of overeager rummage buyers. Many women have no staying power, and you have it in you to beat Cora.

Yours aye,

Flo

152. EMAIL FROM NELL BAKER TO ANGIE GRIFFITHS

The meeting between Robyn and James went OK. If anything, it seems it was a bit of an anticlimax. I'm not sure what Robyn was expecting but it doesn't sound as if James has changed. Apparently they watched *Brief Encounter.* Robyn asked how on earth I didn't realize he was gay.

"Do you mind?" I asked her.

"No," she said. "We talked about the environment. He gave me some books." End of conversation.

I have to say though that she's a bit better. I am beginning to think that maybe Dad has been right all along and that poetry does no good to anyone. Maybe we should all make cakes instead. Some of Mum's cakes were like poems. That lemon sponge that used to melt and just leave the tang of citrus in your mouth. Or the one she did once with rose petals. There was just a slight crunch to the texture when you bit into it. I think that was my favorite, although it made me feel so sad for some reason. Angie, do you think if I'd cooked for Robyn, she would have been OK? Mark says we all go through stages, but I haven't told him about her stealing.

Martin's invited Robyn to Pilgrim House to have tea with him, Dad, and Mrs. Oliver. Maybe that will help. She wasn't going to tell me about it, but luckily he'd copied his letter to me too. Just to make sure everything was aboveboard, he said. I've told her she's to go. And smile. And say yes to whatever anyone asks her to do. Poor kid. I'd almost feel sorry for her if this wasn't all her fault.

153. LETTER FROM MARTIN MORRIS TO MO GRIFFITHS

Dear Mo,

We are going dancing.

Robyn, Mrs. Oliver, George, Nell, Steve, and me.

I am not sure how it quite came about. Things seem to be running away from me these days, just as they used to with Mahad sometimes. I've waited such a long time to get in the photograph, Mo, but now I'm there, it's as if I've walked in the negative by mistake. Nothing is as substantial as it seems.

Anyway, we are to go dancing. George is keen. Mrs. Oliver thinks it is an adventure. Annabel thought it sounded lovely but she's still under house arrest. Brenda doesn't call it that, of course. She says that everyone is just looking after Annabel a bit more. And it would be a shame, it seems, if she doesn't make use of the comfy new sofa and DVD player, which is her son's latest gift to Pilgrim House. Bribery and corruption, Helen *tut-tuts*, but she and Catherine are still there every night, glued to the telly and arguing over the remote control like an old married couple.

So the dancing. Susan was talking at breakfast about how her daughter had taken up salsa. I thought it was some kind of tomato sauce, which made everyone laugh, and then when they explained about the high kicks, I said it sounded just right. All the lovely ladies in Pilgrim House could go with me and show me their panties.

It was only a joke. To be honest, I've taken to talking like this recently because it's easier just to make everyone laugh than to try to remember what people have said. Well, everyone except

Brenda laughed, she came rushing over and said that was enough talk about panties at the breakfast table and, of course, we weren't to go dancing of any kind.

"Why not?" George asked. You know what he's like. As soon as someone says he can't do anything, or instigates a rule he's not personally been responsible for making up, he gets the bit between his teeth.

And it seems there are no actual rules as to why we can't go. Steve said if we really were keen, then he'd come with us to make sure we don't get into "mischief." Mrs. Oliver wants Nell to come so she can play Cupid. And I want Robyn. It's not because she's any use to me anymore. I just like her and the way she's not been broken by what happened.

"You hate me," I said to her the other day, and she looked at me levelly. She comes once a week now to see her granddad so I always make sure I'm somewhere in the hallway and she has to walk past me.

"I don't even think about you," she said. But I could tell it was a lie. She hates me, just as you did toward the end when I wouldn't let you have that one photograph I took of you back. But here's the thing, if you hate, you can still love. If you fear, you can still love. It's when you really don't care that there's no hope. And you never stopped being frightened of me, did you? I bet you were thinking about me right until the end. "A blessed relief," George called your death the other day. "She was so ill. I miss her, of course," he said.

"Of course you do, George," Mrs. Oliver said, patting his hand. They've got awfully pally, those two. They're forever looking up stocks and reading the business pages together. I leave them to it. As far as winning Mrs. Oliver back goes, I've got my own treasure in that envelope under my bed. She's played right into my hands. I just need to wait for the right time to show it to George.

Then we'll see if he's as sympathetic as she might hope. The dancing could be just the ticket time-wise.

"I miss her, of course." As if you were a dog.

He doesn't know what it's like to ache from missing someone. Not like I do. Didn't I always say we should have gone dancing? I took out your photograph, the fists one, the other night, and I held it out and twirled you around the room with me. Steve showed me a few salsa steps after everyone had left the dining room. I think he felt sorry they'd all laughed at me about thinking it was ketchup.

"Could you teach me more?" I asked him. He was about to say no, so I said quickly, "I'll pay you."

So we're to have some private tuition, him and me. It's costing me a fortune, but it'll be worth it when I show everyone up on the dance floor. I'll twirl the ladies around so you can see their panties, and I'll wish they were you. Just you and me in the studio. Having the time of our lives.

M

154. LETTER FROM FLORENCE OLIVER TO LIZZIE CORN

Dear Lizzie,

It was the Seduction Committee I forgot to tell you about in my last letter. I will be forgetting my head next. And it was all my idea too. Or so Martin says. We had a little mutiny over the Residents Committee, I don't mind telling you. George is a lovely man, but I think he might have been allowed to get away with a wee bit much in his marriage. He started making up more and more committee rules until Martin and I said we weren't going to do it anymore. But then Martin thought why not use the committee to matchmake between young Nell and Steve Jenkins.

George wouldn't have to know, and then Robyn could join us, and she didn't have to know either.

So we gave it a go when Robyn came to tea. It was a bit difficult because Robyn kept being rude to Martin even though he's been so good to her, so when we talked about the dancing classes, and Martin said it would be nice if Robyn came too, she made this scoffing noise.

"Hey, manners," I wanted to say, but George got in there first. "You'll say yes, and like it," he said. He looked as surprised as all of us by his words because none of us had been totally sure about going dancing before. But Robyn said she'd come if her mum came too, and Martin and I looked at each other. Things couldn't have worked out better. We hadn't had to do anything, and because George couldn't back out now, Nell would be spending the evening with Steve under our watchful eyes.

Have I told you about the dancing? Things are moving so fast here. It was Susan's idea. Apparently they have classes at the local leisure center and her Mary goes. We were just talking about it at breakfast as a joke, but Brenda believed it, and no one bothered to tell her we weren't serious. And now it seemed serious was exactly what we were.

"You're a genius," Martin whispered to me, when the meeting finished. I wanted to ask him if he'd got my note about the photographs, but George was waiting at the doorway for me to go over the minutes with him. He obviously still thought we'd been having the Residents Committee, which was why he was a bit worried about Robyn being there. He's a stickler for detail.

You were always such a neat dancer. I remember watching you and Graham together once at the Palace. I was sitting on the side, wishing I could be as graceful as you and that I didn't always make Graham angry the way I tried to lead. I'm going to lead in this salsa class though. I'm going to have myself a fine old time, shaking my booty. Just anyone dare to get angry with me anymore.

You'll have to ask young Amy if she can teach you some of the latest dance steps. Susan's great-niece came the other day and she was showing us this dirty dancing they're so fond of nowadays. We did laugh at the way she wriggled her hips, and Amy's such a pretty little thing so I'd bet she'd look even sweeter than Susan's girl did. Even Catherine Francis said it was unusual, which makes me think that maybe Laurie would like it too.

And speaking of hips, my rheumatism's a little worse today. We'll have rain before night falls, you mark my words.

Yours aye,
Flo

155. LETTER FROM GEORGE GRIFFITHS TO BRENDA LEWIS

Dear Brenda,

We have been considering the future of the Pilgrim House Residents Committee and have agreed that it will be acceptable for Steve Jenkins to join us.

However, we would like to have one more meeting to go through some administrative issues first.

Yours sincerely,
George Griffiths

156. EMAIL FROM NELL BAKER TO ANGIE GRIFFITHS (WITH LETTER 141 ATTACHED AND SCANNED)

Hey Angie,

What is this thing you have against Martin? You can't just tell us to stay away from him and not give any explanation. I still don't think you understand what a dear he is. Wait until you come over and then see if you still feel the same. Or tell me what it is you're worried about. Anyway, here's his letter scanned in as you asked. Although I can have no idea why you need to see his handwriting.

It would be difficult anyway to cut off ties right now. We're all going to go dancing together. Even Robyn and Dad. I know, I know. Mark says he's going to pop along just to have a laugh at us.

Robyn was just saying yesterday morning she couldn't see anything in life worth living, and then she comes back from her tea with Martin and Dad to say that she and I are going dancing with them. Now there's a sentence I never thought I'd hear.

Nell

157. NOTE FROM CLAUDE BICHOURIE TO
ANGELA GRIFFITHS

My dear Angela,

No, I cannot get your tickets changed to go immediately. Besides, I will be in Paris for another week and need you with me.

Call me old-fashioned, but I do not think it appropriate for a mother-to-be to rush around without proper planning. Ah, and you thought I did not know. But then of course you forget I am the expert on your body. After all, Angela, I have known it since you were a teenager.

I am delighted. Even if you considered me the last person who needed to know. A little Claude-alini can only bring joy.

I will ask my lawyers to draw you up some papers so I can bring them along tonight for you to sign. Nothing to worry about, we just need to make sure everything is aboveboard, and then you and I will celebrate with a glass of champagne for me, and some sparkling water for Claude-alini's mother.

Until then, keep safe for me.

C

158. NOTE FROM STEVE JENKINS TO MARTIN MORRIS

If you do want a dancing lesson it'll be $35 cash in hand. 4:30, your room.

Cheers,
Steve

159. LETTER FROM MARTIN MORRIS TO MO GRIFFITHS

Dear Mo,

Dancing will be quite different with a woman, I'm sure, but truth is, I didn't quite get the hang of it with Steve. He was a little rougher than he needed to be, and besides, my room is so small. We kept bumping into corners, and once I fell against the bed and hurt my thigh.

I guess I've got out of the habit of touching another person. I wanted to shake him off, although after he went, I got out your photograph again and, as Steve had showed me, I turned around, dipped you down, and then lifted you up again. I could do it all perfectly with you, although my knuckles were white with holding you so tight. I didn't want to let you drop out of my hands, see. Not this time.

"So do you think it'll work?" Mrs. Oliver keeps asking. She means Nell and Steve's seduction. That's why she thinks we're doing it. I'm letting her just get on naturally with George. It's working better now she's not forcing things and frightening him.

But when we were dancing, you and me, I kept getting these shooting pains that went up my arms. They made me breathless.

What if Angie comes back for the dancing? That would be grand, wouldn't it? Another good reason to keep on with the classes. I'll dance with Angie, Nell, and Robyn, and no one will be able to stop me. Then when I've finished with them, I'll capture Mrs. Oliver.

As I twirled you fast round and round, I shut my eyes and thought of you in a red dress, me in a smart suit.

Now George will see what being left alone really feels like.

M

160. ANSWER PHONE MESSAGE FROM
GEORGE GRIFFITHS TO ANGIE GRIFFITHS

Hello Angie,

This is your father speaking. I am sorry I was not here when you rang and I have only just received your message. Brenda gave it to Annabel, who must have mislaid it. It was only when Brenda asked me at breakfast if I had called you back that I found out. We are all getting a little agitated. Martin even dropped his tea for a second time when Brenda was passing on your greetings.

I have been out shopping with Nell. She seemed to think I needed some new clothes. We went to the department store Helen and Catherine are always going on about and it was very clean. Nell might frighten you with some silly stories about how I felt faint in the women's section when she was trying on some dresses, but it was just too long on my feet. Nothing a cup of tea afterward couldn't sort out.

Your sister seems well. Obviously I would prefer it if she could get back with her husband, but at least he seems to be acting more responsibly toward Robyn these days, and perhaps not everyone could be as lucky as I was with your mother. Times change.

Anyway, I am not sure what it is you needed to speak to me about so urgently, but I am here, Angie. Whenever you want me.

George

161. EMAIL FROM NELL BAKER TO ANGIE GRIFFITHS

Hey, Angie, you've been ringing. Don't know why you couldn't leave a proper message but remember your sunglasses when you come. Dad has only got himself a bright red shirt. Yep, that's right. RED. I tried to persuade him to go for something more appropriate but he insisted. We got a black one for Martin too. As a present for the dancing. Admittedly there wasn't much choice, but still.

162. LETTER FROM FLORENCE OLIVER TO LIZZIE CORN

Dear Lizzie,

Well, I don't know! Your letter quite shocked me.

How Laurie expects you to change from just the four of you—her, you, Brian, and Amy—in a four-bedroom house to fit in both Troy and Cora is beyond me. No wonder you were put out. It's quite a different thing from Cora coming for a brief visit to her moving in.

But I'm pleased that Amy chose you to share a room with because it proves that the plan is working, doesn't it? And yes, while I can see it must be annoying to have that disco music playing all the time, soon they will resent Cora for all the restrictions she is putting on them, and you will be the fun one. Tiring though. You are doing the hard work with all those shopping trips and dance moves while all Cora does is play a few games.

And talking of which, we are going dancing tomorrow night. Martin seems quite the thing about it. He and Annabel even did a little two-step thing around the sitting room just now until they knocked Helen's glass of water over. We all expected Brenda to come storming in, but Steve cleared it up without saying anything. He even winked at Martin. "You're an expert," he said, so George and I are even more determined to sit on the sidelines.

"Florence," George said to me as I went up to bed, "I wonder if I could ask you something personal?" I blushed. How long is it since I've done that? No one was in earshot though, so I pretended to be calm. I have come to like his formal ways. I know I found him stuffy to begin with, but it's relaxing after Martin's constant chattering. I'm sure he didn't always used to be so exhausting. Or rude.

"You can," I told George.

Well, he only asked me if I had a red dress. I was puzzled, I can tell you. I suppose it comes from having a daughter in Paris.

So I told him I just had a red coat, and he seemed a bit disappointed, but then wished me a good night.

"Don't let the fleas bite," I told him.

I could have kicked myself when I got back here. As if George is the type to talk about fleas with. What will he think of me?

Glad Laurie is thawing a bit. Trust me, pet. Things will work out.

Yours aye,
Flo

163. EMAIL FROM NELL BAKER TO ANGIE GRIFFITHS

No, Angie, you'll have to do better than "*trust me.*"

I thought we'd finished with all this.

Is it because Dad and I are finally having a relationship of some sort that you don't like? Or I'm having some fun of my own at last?

You are the one who ran away fifteen years ago and have been home, what, about three times since. So what gives you the right to start bossing us all around now?

Perhaps the same mystery objection that wouldn't let you talk to Mum for all those years? Not even when we all begged you to come and see her at the end.

Come on, Angie, this fantasy life you're living in Paris might be wonderful, but some of us have to live in the real world. Going salsa dancing with Dad might not be the most glamorous evening, but don't try and spoil even that for me. You're going to be a mother soon and it's about time you grew up. If you've something to say, get on a plane and come and say it to me. Then I'll listen to you.

Nell

164. LETTER FROM MARTIN MORRIS TO MO GRIFFITHS

Dear Mo,

Well, we went.

I don't think it was quite what any of us were expecting. Not even Steve. Although to be honest, being squashed in the back of his car while Florence luxuriated in the front seat probably didn't help start the evening off on the best of footings. That, and the dreadful Spanish music he insisted on playing. Florence kept tapping her fingers on Steve's arm and saying this was the life, but I just couldn't see it myself. What I didn't know was why I couldn't have gone with George in Nell's car, but it seemed they were to be just family. I couldn't help wonder if that was Robyn's idea.

If only she knew.

Anyway, by the time we got to the hall, they were still taking down the badminton nets and there was a smell of sneakers that made me want to sit down. All I could see were these low benches though, so I tried to jiggle from foot to foot to keep the blood flowing in my legs.

"Getting ready are you, Martin?" Florence said, elbowing me. I frowned at her. We could see Nell and George on the other side of the hall, but Florence didn't seem to be making any rush to move. She nudged me again to look where Robyn was draped backward over a man's arm. We could see her upside-down face before she was flung upright and twirled around to dip the other side. It looked painful.

"Yahoo," Nell called to us, waving her arm.

"You go on," Florence said, nudging Steve forward. I felt sympathetic toward him, but not when he turned around and winked at me.

"Remember the steps," he said.

"Remember what steps?" Mrs. Oliver is like a terrier who can't leave anything alone. "You haven't been having secret lessons, have you?"

I shook my head, and held out my arm to her. "Will you do me the honor," I said, and when she took it, I carried on, "of showing me your panties tonight?"

"Oh Martin," she squeezed my hand painfully. "You are a card."

It seems this is what is expected of me lately. To be the dirty old man. I wish I was back in the news agency with Mahad, working together in silence.

It felt like a long walk over to where George and Nell were standing, deep in conversation next to a young couple, dressed in jeans and sweaters and holding hands. Steve was squatting down next to a portable CD player.

"There's no music," Nell said, but just then Robyn came back with her partner. He was about five foot six, and at least sixty years old. He let go of Robyn to tuck his shirt into his tightly belted trousers, and I noticed to my horror we were wearing exactly the same black shirt. George had got me it from town and I knew it was ridiculous, but I thought the others would see the joke. Trouble is no one laughed.

"I am Phillipo," he said, waving his heavily bejeweled fingers at us as Robyn ran around to her mother's side. "Your teacher. We will do the imagining tonight. And what is music anyway but a dream of the mind."

I could hear Florence scoffing next to me. "We were better off in your car listening to the real stuff," she told Steve. "At least it was less smelly there too."

Robyn was still red-faced from the dancing. "You look hot," I said to her, but she ignored me.

"Granddad," she said, turning to George, "will you dance with me? You look so smart, all dressed up in red."

Just then there was a commotion at the door, and Nell's policeman walked in. "Mark," Nell cried, and went running over. Florence caught my eye, and we looked to where Steve was still fiddling with the music player. It was very disappointing.

"Shall I get my CD?" Steve asked, and before I could say anything, he'd left.

"Line up, line up." Phillipo clapped his hands now, and Florence took George by the hand, and Nell and Mark stood together. Only me and Robyn were left. I was thinking that was a bit of all right, but she went and ruined it by going to sit on the bench.

"I'm dancing with Steve," she said. "We arranged it."

By whom, I wanted to ask, a minute ago you were begging your granddad to dance with you, but George was comparing the time on his wristwatch with the gym clock, so I knew he wouldn't accuse Robyn of having bad manners. Besides, Florence wasn't going to let him go.

"I'll sit the first one out," I said in what I hoped was a gracious way. As Steve came back clutching his wretched CD, Phillipo clicked his fingers at shoulder height. He walked sideways, his upper body seesawing and I could hear him shouting above Steve's music. "The tango is from the streets. It is not polite. It is most of all a dance about the *passiono*."

From the yelp George gave, I guessed Florence had just pinched him. Despite the $35 I'd spent on lessons, I was glad to be sitting this out. Steve and I hadn't talked much about the *pas-*

siono when we were practicing in my room. The young couple were looking very nervous too.

"Remember it is your hearts which are touching," Phillipo said, "not your bodies."

I wanted to be back in my little bedroom, thinking about you and me, and our hearts touching. I shut my eyes and when I opened them again, everyone was in different parts of the hall.

"I've got more than enough passion to go around, thank you very much," Florence was shouting, as Phillipo clutched at her waist. I could see George's face and I was pleased how he looked as if he was in agony. He'd told me all about his back, so I could imagine what it was costing him standing straight like that. It would have made you laugh, seeing him and Florence and thinking about hearts touching.

"You are in the Buenos Aires, you are in the bull fighters, you are in love, you are in hate," Phillipo kept shouting.

"Just hate," I wanted to shout. I wondered what George's expression would be like when I showed him Florence's photographs. I knew it was the next step, now that they didn't seem to be able to take their eyes off each other.

Only Robyn and Steve looked as if they knew what they were doing. At least they were the only ones moving in some kind of circle. The young couple kept bumping into Nell and Mark, and Florence and George were just standing there now, holding hands and swaying a bit. The smell of furniture polish gave me a sudden urge to be sick.

"Dip, dip, dive," that bloody Phillipo was yelling. "Feel the grass under the feet."

"Want me to take you around so you don't feel like such a wall-flower?" Steve shouted across the hall at me, and I could see Robyn laughing as he whispered something to her. I shut my eyes again, and ran my finger around the collar of my stupid black shirt. I wanted only you and me to have been there.

At last, the music came to an end and I thought at last we could all go home, have a nice cup of tea, and forget about it. But then more music started up again. Florence and George hobbled over. "My hips are agony," Florence said. "What a shame you didn't get to dance, Martin."

I shrugged, trying to look as if I didn't care. "Dancing's not really my thing," I said. "Not public displays anyway."

"Hey Martin." Robyn was whirling by now, she almost looked pretty when her face was moving. "Pity you couldn't find a partner, especially when you've been having lessons."

I looked down at the ground.

"She's a little overexcited," George said. "I've had enough anyway. I don't know about you, Florence, but I'll get Nell to take us home." He shuffled over to where Nell and Mark were trying out steps on their own in the corner.

"What will that girl think of to lie about next?" I said to Florence, and she gave me a funny look.

"Well, I enjoyed it and George is a good dancer," she said, as if that had anything to do with anything.

Nell came bustling over. "You won't mind if I just drop you off and then come back," she said. "It's just that—" She shrugged and looked over at Mark.

I didn't care. All I wanted was my little room at the top of the house. Our little sanctuary. Yours and mine.

"Good-bye, Granddad," Robyn shouted. "You're a lovely, lovely dancer."

"That he is," Florence shouted back. "Lovely."

It was an unfortunate end to the evening that George should stumble just then on the way out of the door. I could see Robyn stare at me when she came running over, but as Florence kept saying as Steve took us home, it was just bad luck he fell over my foot and at least Nell was there to pick him up and take him to the emergency.

And now I can't get rid of that dreadful music from my head. It wasn't at all what I imagined. A classy woman like you would have hated it. We should have black ties and dinner suits. Music we could hold each other decently to.

At least George won't be in any state to go dancing again for a while. Brenda has just come knocking on my door to say it was a sprained ankle. She seemed to think I might care.

M

165. LETTER FROM FLORENCE OLIVER TO LIZZIE CORN

Dear Lizzie,

Well, I suppose I could ask if you could come and stay here if things got too bad at Laurie's, but there's no actual bedroom available and as you pointed out when I wanted to stay with you, we're a bit old for put-me-ups. I can't imagine Annabel will be moving out again soon because her sons are so generous. They gave us a new coffeemaker the other day. I would have stroked its shiny surface if I'd have got there first, but it's streaked from where the others have had a go.

I'm not sure I'd be brave enough to use it ever. Steve demonstrated it for us, and although he made us laugh by pretending to make the *whoosh-whoosh* noises himself, it's too much like a space machine for me. And of course coffee does such dreadful things to my insides.

Are you sure you couldn't stick it out there? I know it's not nice that Troy told Amy you were wicked after she did her dancing display, and Brian should not be blackmailing you for giving him nightmares after the sword stories, but it is still your home. What a shame you decided against Bournemouth when Cora first moved in and you felt you needed to be there. It would have been a good break, but I can't leave George right now.

He's fine after his nasty accident but it's nice for him to be looked after a bit. What fools we were to go dancing, and although, Lizzie, we only stood up together for a bit and it was George Griffiths, I got a tingle. I really did. And I think he did too. I told him he was a perfect leader.

Let me know if things get better, and if they don't, I promise I'll ask Brenda about the possibilities of a bed and breakfast for you locally.

Yours aye,
Flo

166. EMAIL FROM NELL BAKER TO ANGIE GRIFFITHS

Hey Angie,

OK, I will wait to get your letter, but I can't imagine what it will say that will make me change my mind about Martin. I feel rather sorry for him actually. He hated the dancing, and I think his nose was put out of joint with Dad and Florence Oliver doing so well at it. Did you ever suspect Dad of having any natural rhythm? Funny, because Mum always hated it so much, didn't she?

Dad's ankle is less swollen now, and he's looking forward to seeing you. Robyn's perked up too. She's been seeing more of her father, and Steve at Pilgrim House has taken her under his wing to help run this youth club of his. It gives me a bit more time. I'd like you to meet Mark.

Nell

167. ANSWER PHONE MESSAGE FROM
GEORGE GRIFFITHS TO ANGIE GRIFFITHS

Hello Angie,

This is your father talking to your machine. Wretched ankle. It spoiled the whole evening for us, but Florence has been a saint.

She says she has an ulterior mission to get me ready for dancing again, and I must say I might rather look forward to it.

Mind you, I wonder what it would be like to go to Buenos Aires. It's such a shame your mother never liked to travel, but we had some good holidays in Bethington, didn't we?

Actually, Angie, I never really liked it there. The sea was always so cold, and the only advantage I could see was that it was miles from anywhere. No one we knew had ever heard of it, but your mother said that was what she liked.

I'm not speaking ill here, Angie. She was a marvelous mother. We were all so lucky. The doctor says I should be walking fine by the time you come. All I need is a bit of rest. Poor Martin is blaming himself. He has made a big speech about spending some time with me later this afternoon. He says he has something to show me.

And this has been your father.

168. LETTER FROM FLORENCE OLIVER TO LIZZIE CORN

Dear Lizzie,

And you thought you had miseries. I wish my life was over.

Why do I always persist in thinking I am the type of person good things can happen to? Didn't Graham always tell me how I spoiled things?

Martin has shown George those photographs he took of me.

"Why did you do that?" I asked him. I'd gone to take George a nice cup of tea because he can't move far after his accident, and Martin was just coming out of the room. All I can think about was slipping off my blouse to show my back.

What will George think of me?

"I thought it might cheer him up," Martin said, "but he just wants to be left alone."

I went to go past Martin into George's room, but Martin stopped me. "He particularly doesn't want to see you," he said.

I spilled the tea then. Left the cup on the floor and the liquid blooming into a stain on the carpet. I ran back here and lay down on the bed. I've only just managed to get up. I shall have to leave, of course. I can't bear how Catherine and Helen will look at me. And Robyn and Nell too. Just as we were getting on so well. And I've no sons to buy expensive kitchen equipment and keep my place.

George particularly didn't want to see me. As if I'm shameful.

But when Martin was taking the photographs, it didn't feel like that, Lizzie. It didn't feel dirty or stupid or anything bad. It felt like my last chance to prove that life was still worth living.

Well, it's not now.

How did we mess everything up so? Perhaps we needed Graham and Frank to keep us in order more than we thought.

It's that which hurts more than nearly everything.

Yours aye,

Flo

169. LETTER FROM MARTIN MORRIS TO MO GRIFFITHS

Dear Mo,

The last few months here, surrounded by memories of you, have been the happiest of my life, and now with Angie coming, it looks set to get even happier. I should have trusted you all along. It's as if you sent me here to find out about Angie and give us a final chance to be together.

And I appreciate that, angel.

I just wish I could feel a bit more enthusiastic about it. I sit in my chair for hours at a time, not even getting the old photographs out. Not even writing to you properly on paper. Just in my mind. Telling you again and again everything that we've been through together. From the minute you walked into my studio and told me I wasn't going to get your clothes off.

I bet Florence is wishing she'd kept to that. You didn't think I'd let her have George, did you? Everything would be working out perfectly if it wasn't for all the fuss and attention George is getting with his stupid foot. Somehow I wasn't expecting that.

I have one more card to play though. I have Tricia.

M

170. NOTE FROM CLAUDE BICHOURIE TO ANGIE GRIFFITHS

Dear Angela,

The lawyer has passed on your recent communication and, even despite your increasingly strange behavior, I am at a loss to understand what is happening. Are you now saying this child is not mine? Do you have proof of this? You understand that these are not matters that can be treated purely emotionally, I hope.

I will come to your flat this afternoon to discuss this with you. Please be there this time. You are no longer a child who can run away from difficult situations.

Claude

171. EMAIL FROM NELL BAKER TO ANGIE GRIFFITHS

Nope, your letter didn't come this morning either, but I can't go to Martin's room and hunt around for some papers you say might be there. Who do you think I am? First Robyn gets caught stealing from him, and then me. People will really start to think we've gone mad. And what would I be looking for? Honestly, Angie, you will have to tell me more.

172. NOTE FROM FLORENCE OLIVER TO
GEORGE GRIFFITHS
(ATTACHED TO THE FILE CONTAINING
THE RESIDENTS COMMITTEE MINUTES)

Dear George,

I know you don't want to see me, and I can understand why, but I am a silly woman and not a bad one.

I have never had pictures like that taken of me before. The only other person to see me naked was my husband. And that's why, if you can imagine, I wanted to have it done once. Just to see what it felt like.

Well, I know now.

I am returning the minutes from the Residents Committee meetings. I am presuming you will no longer want me as secretary.

Florence

173. ANSWER PHONE MESSAGE FROM
NELL BAKER TO ANGIE GRIFFITHS

OK, this one time I will do it. But you can't keep hiding, Angie. You will have to explain everything soon.

174. NOTE FROM ROBYN BAKER TO STEVE JENKINS

Hey Steve,

Granddad has asked me to let you have the minutes of the Residents Committee. He says he's too tired to do it anymore, but he said to tell you, and I quote, "Mrs. Oliver has proved herself to be exceptional at organization." Coming from Granddad, that's almost a declaration of love!

Rob

175. LETTER FROM MARTIN MORRIS TO MO GRIFFITHS

Dear Mo,

So it seems you are not the only member of your family who can't leave me alone. I came back to my room this morning to find Nell here, looking anxious.

"Are you waiting for me, dear?" I asked, but I was trying to sneak a glance under the bed at the same time, to check nothing had been disturbed. You know what I am like about people snooping around me. It wasn't the same as when I caught Robyn because that was all part of my plan.

Nell nodded and I beckoned to her to sit on the chair. I took the bed, although this put me at a disadvantage as my feet didn't touch the floor. I have taken to lying on the bed, my head propped up by pillows for hours, but this didn't seem appropriate when there was someone else in the room.

"So what is it?" I asked, but she didn't seem to have anything to say. I waited as patiently as I could. I even laced my fingers together in the way George does. The trouble with Nell is that every time I see her I think of the little girl having her hair brushed on my studio stool. Surely she must have some memory of me. I'm waiting for her to recognize me. To prove I did exist all those years ago.

"I was wondering if you knew my mother," she said then. I was so shocked at how she must have read my mind that I just stared at her open-mouthed.

And that was when I should have told her everything. Should have talked about how she came to my studio with her mother one day many years ago. I should have asked her if she knew that her mother looked out of the window most evenings, half-knowing, half-hoping I would be there.

But I didn't. I just said, "And how could I?"

To which, of course, she had no reply. She stood up, brushed her skirt from under her, and I wanted to call her back then, to tell her everything, because that's exactly the gesture you used to make, but I couldn't speak. I need to wait for Angie. She's the one I need to tell all this to.

It was only as Nell was going, I noticed the top of my box of letters to you was half-opened, but by then it was too late. At least, Angie will understand everything.

M

176. EMAIL FROM NELL BAKER TO ANGIE GRIFFITHS

Of course Martin never knew Mum. I asked him straight out. It was awful. He came back when I was in his room, and because he thought I was looking for him, I had to listen to him explain how important we've all been for him. Even Robyn, he kept saying. He's a good man, Angie. I can't understand you at all. And yes, I've got a piece of his handwriting now, although it's just an envelope with a woman's name on it. Mo. You're not expecting me to open his letter, are you?

Time to stop these silly games, Angie. Mum was never frightened of anyone, let alone Martin. Just as Robyn isn't. She'd tell me if she was. Although I was surprised to find a folder with Robyn's name in Martin's room. I didn't have time to look inside and I would have taken that too if he hadn't come back just then. It's probably just some of her poems from when they were working together. I'll ask her about it. She's been back to dancing, did I tell you? Steve took his youth group, and Robyn joined them. The last thing I want is for you to fill her head with fanciful thoughts. Not now, when she's really coming out of her shell.

177. **LETTER FROM FLORENCE OLIVER TO LIZZIE CORN**

Dear Lizzie,

And just when I thought my heart couldn't break any more, George is back in the hospital. He was taken there last night, and no one will say what's wrong.

But I know.

It's my fault. I have shocked him to death with my photographs. He couldn't even bring himself to talk to me, although I've heard he passed the file about the Residents Committee back to Brenda with a note saying he didn't want to be involved anymore.

And now his empty room is just as Annabel's room was when she'd gone, but doubly so. I'm not sure if any of us realized how much Pilgrim House *was* about George. I've noticed we've all been filling in his charts with how many cups of tea we have. Even how many biscuits we've eaten. If only we'd done this before.

"It'll be his ankle," Susan said, staring at me as if that was my fault too because of the dancing. I can't look at Martin. We all are keeping to ourselves as much as we can.

So, Lizzie, if George stays in the hospital, there may indeed be a room for you here after all. But it's not exactly how we would have wanted it, is it?

Florence

178. **ANSWER PHONE MESSAGE FROM**
NELL BAKER TO ANGIE GRIFFITHS

Hey Angie,

I've just come back from the hospital and it's going to be OK. Dad's going to pull through. Oh, I'm sorry to be crying. It's just such a relief. They told me to come home for some food and sleep. I didn't want to, but the nurse promised he'd be fine. I'll go back after lunch.

Angie, stop this nonsense about Martin. Please. It's not the right time.

We need to talk about more important things like why you find it so difficult to come home and why you stopped talking to Mum. Whatever it was that happened, tell me about it.

What on earth could be so bad for you here?

Your letter has come, by the way. I'll open it after I've had a bath. I'm exhausted. Dad looked so little lying there in the hospital bed. When Mum was ill at the end, I felt that her death finally gave her back to us. As if her last days were so bad and painful that they took all the good memories of her away, and it was only when she died that I didn't need to feel guilty anymore.

But it's different with Dad. We're only just getting to know him. I feel like Robyn must have felt when she used to stamp her feet and say "it's not fair."

OK, long bath now and then I'll read your letter. Promise.

Nell

179. LETTER FROM ANGIE GRIFFITHS TO NELL BAKER (ATTACHED TO LETTER 180)

Dear Nell,

This won't be easy for you, but when you read this letter, you'll see why I didn't want to tell you about it by email. I'm sure that the M of this letter is Martin. In which case, it can't be a coincidence that he turns up in Dad's home and suddenly everything changes.

I never spoke to Mum about it. What could I say? I think she knew I found the letter because she never chased me after I'd gone to Paris and made it clear I didn't want to speak to her. I used to long for her to come after me at the beginning so she could give me a proper explanation for it all, but then I came to terms with the fact she was probably too ashamed. Of course, by then I'd met Claude and she didn't have my address, but even so, she had no right to keep something like this from me.

I guess you can understand now why I didn't want to come home. What would I have ever said to Dad? Although, sometimes I used to wonder if Dad was like how he was because of what happened. And me too. I'm not proud of who I've become.

Because look at the date on the letter, Nell. What if it wasn't just a brief affair Mum got caught up in, but something with lasting consequences? If you do the math, it matches completely with my birth date. Now you see why I had to go. Anyway, it feels good to share this now. And more important too now that I've got little tadpole inside me.

And no, in answer to your earlier question, I'm not sure if it's Claude's or not. There might even be a strange photographer who has that honor. Well, they do say like mother, like daughter, don't they? Anyway, now you see why I want you to keep Martin away from Robyn and Dad. And stay away yourself.

Love from your sister,

Angie

180. LETTER FROM MARTIN MORRIS TO MO GRIFFITHS (DATED 15 SEPTEMBER 1974)

Dear Mo,

You make it sound almost easy.

You think it's best we don't see each other anymore. It will cause too much pain for too many people. After all, parting won't kill us, and we can be friends. You'll have a special place in your heart for me.

Really. Well, what about me? Don't I get a say in all this?

I love you, Mo. From the minute you came into my studio—and let's remember that, it was *you* who walked into *my* life—I have known my North. It is wherever you are.

Don't think you can walk out on me like this. That it won't kill us. That I'll want to rest just in the "special place" you keep for me, tucked away from everything good and clean. I'm not a dirty secret, or a memory you will take out sometimes and smile over.

I will never stop loving you. You are me, and I am you. Apart from you, I am nothing, not even half. You are my sweetheart shot to my heart.

I will follow you, Mo, wherever you go. Even years from now, you will look out of your window and see me there. You will go and pick up your mail and my letter will be waiting. You will open a magazine and see my photographs.

Let's talk about pain then, shall we?

Come and see me. I deserve that at least. I will be in the studio all week.

M

181. LETTER FROM MARTIN MORRIS TO MO GRIFFITHS

Dear Mo,

George is in the hospital again and I have just been to see him.

I didn't mean to. It was just that I was hanging around reception when Brenda suddenly bundled me into her car saying she couldn't bear how upset I was about George, so although she shouldn't, she'd take me to the hospital. I didn't disagree because I thought I might enjoy the visit. Florence seems to think it's his last few days on earth if her wailing and moaning is anything to go by, and if so, then I wanted to tell him about us.

But then, halfway there I looked across at Brenda crouched

over the wheel pushing the car to go even faster, and it struck me that if he went before me, then he would get to you first.

It would be like the dancing. One false step, and I'd be back on the substitute's bench.

But I needn't have worried. He wasn't quite sitting up in bed, but he was awake enough to raise his hand when I walked in. There was a chair already drawn up, but no sign of Nell or Robyn. I looked around for a card from Angie, but there wasn't anything. Not even a flower or a grape. Just bleeping machines in every corner.

I sat down, and he nodded at me. He looked as if the oxygen had been sucked out of him till he was just a husk. It was hard to imagine how this man could ever have had the power to stop me getting what I wanted.

"So how's the ankle?" I asked. "Brenda's been at us about going against her advice with the dancing."

It seemed everyone had a different theory for George's illness. Me, I thought he was just being bloody-minded. Now, it wasn't just the fact of you and him getting together in heaven that was worrying me, but if he died and Angie came over for the funeral, then it would spoil the excitement of her picking me over him as her dad.

"Bring me them," he asked as I got up to go. He had to gesture to me to lean right over him so I could hear. His voice was little more than a whisper.

"Bring you what?" I knew what he meant but I wanted him to beg.

"Trisha's sweetheart shots," he said, and then his head fell right back. He shut his eyes. "But please, please don't tell anyone about me and her. Not Nell, or Angie."

This was all I needed so I straightened up, trying not to wince, and took his hand. "I will, George," I said extra loudly so Brenda could hear me. I knew she was standing outside looking through the window, only half able to give us the "privacy" she went on about because she was enjoying the moment so much.

On the way home, I said George had wanted to see me again.

"Of course he does, Martin," she said. "You've been such friends. It's been very nice indeed to see you bonding." And she wiped away a tear.

I must admit I felt like having a good weep myself. Imagine two old men, reaching their last years and finally finding the friendship they never quite managed before in their lives. One a respectable accountant, and one a would-be pornographer. What on earth could they have in common? But that's the marvelous thing about preparing to die. It strips away all the useless bits and lets us concentrate on what is really important. What's at our core.

I knew this would be a story Brenda would tell many times in the future, and she'd top it off by describing how she saw me and George squeezing hands at our farewell.

Because what on earth do me and George have in common, Mo? Yes, it's enough to make you weep.

M

182. EMAIL FROM NELL BAKER TO ANGIE GRIFFITHS

So let's get this straight. You found this letter in Mum's drawers about fifteen years ago and have never told me.

How could you, Angie? You had no right. And it's not just because she is my mother and Dad is my father too, and whatever sham this letter makes our family is my sham too, but because you are my sister.

It hurt so much when you disappeared without giving a reason. Don't you know how much it would have helped to know what was going on? That it wasn't just my little sister doing one of her huffy fits.

If you'd have told me the truth then, I could have done something. We could have gone to see Mum and Dad and sorted it out together. We could have done a very un-Griffiths thing and had it out in the open. And then none of us would have had to live under its shadow for the rest of our lives.

And now you say casually you don't know who the father of your baby is. Get real, Angie. Take a long hard look at yourself. You can't just drift in and out of all our lives anymore as if you don't matter. You do.

It's Mum I feel sorry for here. She must have been so scared.

183. NOTE FROM CLAUDE BICHOURIE TO ANGELA GRIFFITHS

Dear Angela,

My lawyers have informed me that you have returned my last maintenance check and told them that you will be returning to England with no known address at present.

I am writing to you through them because you have not been replying to my last notes, and I want to warn you that I am not prepared to lose my child without a battle. Or you. Do you really imagine I will believe in a fairy tale about you meeting a photographer and this being his child?

We may have started with a business arrangement, Angie, and if we have to end with one, that will make me sad, but not as sad as no arrangement at all.

I expect you to make contact with my office at least.

184. LETTER FROM MARTIN MORRIS TO MO GRIFFITHS

Dear Mo,

Well, I didn't get my second visit to George after all. Steve came up while I was waiting for Brenda in reception, my shoebox carefully wrapped up in a carrier bag.

"Brenda's not coming," he said. He started shuffling through some papers, but I could tell he was watching for my reaction. Things have been a bit difficult between us since the dancing, although I don't see why it should be him who is aggrieved. He pocketed my $35 sharp enough. I can't help wondering if Robyn has said something.

"But we were going to the hospital," I told him. "George is wanting to see me."

"Apparently he's not anymore," Steve said. He looked up, his finger keeping place in a sheaf of expense forms. I couldn't help thinking how George would have itched to sort them out. Do one of his magic filing thingies on them. "Nell asked particularly that he has no visitors apart from family."

"And Brenda agreed?"

"Yes. She had a long conversation with Nell this morning. Apparently, Mrs. Baker was very upset."

It didn't make sense. Nell has always been on my side, and I thought of Brenda's tears in the car on our last visit. I should have known better than to trust women.

"And Florence? Is she allowed to go to the hospital?" I knew I was sounding sarcastic, but I was annoyed. I'd got her photograph in my bag, love, along with yours. It was going to be my moment. First Trisha, and then I was going to show him Florence, and then finally you. I thought I might even say something about Angie, if the time was right.

"Mrs. Oliver? No, she's in her room. She's very upset."

"We all are." I shifted the bag I was holding from one hand to the other. I had a sudden vision of all the photographs tumbling out over the reception floor. Yours on top. "Oh," I was going to say to George when I passed it over to him, almost as if I'd forgotten it was in there, "that was taken at the same shoot as Trisha's."

But Steve had gone back to his paperwork, and there was nothing for me to do but to go back to my room.

I stopped at the doorway, though. "He will be all right, won't he?" I asked.

"We're all going to die eventually, Martin," Steve said. And I caught a flash of his knuckles as he turned a page over. Was it the hand with love or hate on it? I couldn't make it out.

I stopped in at George's room on the way up to mine. Stood there for a few minutes, looking for something I could take, but the picture of you had gone. Nell must have taken it to the hospital. Also the ones of her and Angie. I would have liked another one of Angie.

I caught sight of a bottle of whiskey that Nell had given him once, and pocketed that instead.

And now here I am back in my room, writing this letter to you and preparing to wait all over again. I should be good at this, but somehow it gets harder and harder. The whiskey bottle keeps looking back at me. One small drink won't hurt.

M

185. LETTER FROM DR. CROFT TO BRENDA LEWIS

Dear Brenda,

I went to visit Martin Morris in the hospital today.

Personally, I'm convinced that his abuse of alcohol was a one-off, but I can see it upset the other residents and understand your reservations. I do think, however, that it would be an act of kindness to keep his room open for him until a final decision is reached.

I've arranged for him to move to a nursing home nearer to my office until we know exactly what the position is.

Yours sincerely,
Michael Croft

186. **LETTER FROM FLORENCE OLIVER TO LIZZIE CORN**

Dear Lizzie,

Do you remember when, at one of those military dinners, there was a red-faced officer who told us a story from his school-days about how a teacher had, for some reason, lent him a book. The officer had loved it so much that he scribbled in the margins by accident. He knew that when he got into class the next day, his crime would be discovered and he'd have a whipping at the least. So he prayed. He was only a little boy, but he got on his knees and prayed and prayed that there would be a miracle and something would happen so he wouldn't be found out.

In the morning, he checked the book and the scribbles were still there. Disaster. He pretended he was ill at breakfast, but his mother said he had to go to school. She even drove him there to make sure he was all right. Double disaster. Sitting in the front seat of her car, feeling the book like a ticking bomb in his satchel, he looked out for the smoke that would let him know his school had burned down. The sky was clear. Double double disaster.

And when he walked into the classroom, the headmaster was waiting. This was worse than the boy feared. He was sure everyone knew what he had done. "I have some very distressing news," the headmaster said when the class were all seated. The boy slumped down on his desk. "Mrs. Campbell passed away in the night."

There was an excited commotion in the classroom. The boy found it hard to understand. Passed away. Passed where? And then he realized. The teacher had died. He burst out crying. Everyone stopped talking and stared at him, but he couldn't say how his prayers were responsible for her murder because then he'd have to go to prison. He ran out of the classroom and all the way home, stopping only to throw the wretched book into the river. When he got home, his mother was there. She took one look at his face and put him to bed, apologizing all the time for not be-lieving him when he said he was ill.

That's what I feel like now, Lizzie.

You see, Martin has been taken away. No one is sure whether he is coming back or not. They found him drunk in George's empty room, covering the walls with the photographs of naked women.

"You were up there," Annabel said at breakfast, pointing at me. Susan smiled at me and shook her head slightly so I tried to smile back. "You're a saucy lady like the four and twenty virgins," Annabel went on.

Helen squeezed my arm. "Just humor her," she said. "It's a kindness." So in the brightest voice I could muster, I said, "Yes, Annabel, Martin took my photograph with no clothes too," and she nodded, satisfied. As well she might. Helen winked at me, and God help me, I winked back.

I crept into Martin's room this afternoon. I was looking for my envelope and I found it eventually, tucked under some library books. It had hardly been opened but it wasn't the same envelope Martin had in his hand when he left George's room. So if Martin hadn't shown George my photographs, then what had he shown him? Whose photograph could be so bad that it would put George in the hospital?

There was a file with Robyn's name on it. I took that too, and the box of letters. Remember the mystery envelopes the home help told us about? Mo, that was the name of the woman Martin's been writing to. Poor sod. I wonder if she ever wished Martin dead. Somehow I guessed so.

That officer, at the dinner table, the one who killed his teacher, what he said after, during coffee, when I asked him, was that he never regretted his prayers. And it was this that he was the most ashamed of. Not the scribbling, or the death. He was so re-lieved at his escape after the initial shock that he even wished he'd kept the book.

There was something cold about Martin's room. I was glad to shut the door.

Yours aye,
Flo

187. LETTER FROM CLAUDE BICHOURIE TO ANGELA GRIFFITHS

Dear Angela,

I have been to see your photographer. It took some time to discover who he was, but you should know by now I nearly always get what I want.

He gave me your photographs. He is little more than a child, Angela, but I have to applaud you on your choice. He is an artist. The shots are beautiful. I paid him in full, fuller than full because I wanted him to know he was selling more than just a negative.

"Mrs. Griffiths would like to have no more contact with you," I told him, and he nodded. "No more contact at all, whatever happens," I repeated, just to make sure he got the message.

He nodded again. And I added some more notes on the pile just for good measure.

So that's that. The child is now all mine.

Go to England, and then come back home to me. We will talk properly. I promise.

Claude

188. NOTE FROM FLORENCE OLIVER TO ROBYN BAKER

Dear Robyn,

Come and see me in my room after you've seen your granddaddy, love. I have something of yours and I'd rather give it to you in person. Besides, I could do with a break. Your granddaddy is a demanding patient now that he is getting better. He had Steve bring in his tango music the other day. You will have to come and dance for us. Steve said you knew all the steps now.

Yours,
Florence

189. LETTER FROM GEORGE GRIFFITHS TO BRENDA LEWIS

Dear Brenda,

I am still at a loss to understand why you painted my room without consulting me during my brief stay in the hospital.

Nell tells me I should be grateful and I am trying to be, and indeed it is true that magnolia is a color that does not offend. However, I did take the liberty while in the hospital of drafting a Residents Charter, and it feels that this might be an appropriate time to discuss this with you.

I have asked Nell to type it, as Mrs. Oliver tells me that you had difficulty reading the minutes from our inaugural committee meeting, and it would be a shame for this not to get a proper consultation.

And lest you think I am always complaining, I would like to say it is good to be back.

Yours sincerely,
George Griffiths

190. EMAIL FROM NELL BAKER TO
    ANGIE GRIFFITHS
    (WITH LETTER 191 SCANNED AND ATTACHED)

Dear Angie,

Martin has left Pilgrim House. I'd already told Brenda we didn't want him seeing Dad anymore. It got a bit awkward because she kept gushing on about what nice friends they were, so I said Dad was upset about the photographs.

"What photographs?" she asked, so I told her how Martin had been showing Dad photographs of nude women and upsetting him.

She didn't believe me at first, but then, apparently Martin got drunk and posted the pictures all around Dad's room. Mrs. Oliver said Steve had called it a shrine to women. How strange is that? In Dad's room too. It messed up the walls, so Steve had to paint them, which of course Dad's complaining about.

Brenda keeps apologizing now. "Your father is the ticking heart of Pilgrim House," she says, so I don't mention all the times she complained about him interfering. Robyn's been going to his room to read him Mum's poems, and because Dad can't move he's had to listen to them. Serves him right for not listening to Mum first time around.

Do you want to see Martin? I'll come with you if you do. You don't have to do anything on your own anymore. I promise you that.

Here's the letter I picked up in his room that time. I wasn't sure whether to show it to you or not. It's pretty grim reading because it looks as if Mum hid the baby (you) from him. Still, I thought if there was the chance he was my dad and I'd had so many secrets kept from me, then I'd want to know everything. There's a whole box of other letters from him to Mum, you know. I'll go and get them. I feel so sorry for her. And you, of course.

                                                                Nell

191. LETTER FROM MARTIN MORRIS TO
       MO GRIFFITHS (DATED 16 MAY 1975)

Dear Mo,

You'll be tired after your picnic in the park today. Did you see me? You kept looking over at the trees as if you were hoping I'd come out, but I was enjoying just being able to watch you without anyone bothering us.

It was restful with the sun on my face. Some days when I'm stuck in the shop I don't get to feel the weather much at all. Mahad has a fan on the counter that he switches on, and it used to swing from side to side, but he's fixed it so it just blows where he's standing now. I don't mind. When he's there, I don't do much. He prefers to deal with customers himself.

I'll venture out if there's a chance I might see you, but there's no point otherwise. I'll go back up to the studio if it gets awkward. Sometimes Mahad has business associates he wants to talk to without me. The studio is just the same as it was the first time you came. A few more photographs of different women all curling up at the edges now, and you'll probably find it dustier because it doesn't get the regular cleanup the girls would do, but there's still a mattress in the corner, and the table with two chairs around it. I lie on the bed and look up at the ceiling and wait until I hear Mahad calling back up for me.

"Don't you have any friends?" he asks me. "What's happened to the big ladies' man you used to be? Don't tell me you've got a heart to get broken."

I smile. We don't really talk, Mahad and me, although he gets a cruel streak about him sometimes. He'll ask why I've no backbone, no gumption, what it is about English men that makes them so weak. I ignore him when he's in those moods because just as quickly it will blow over. Then I'll go back behind the counter and take my seat and he'll turn the fan back to him, and another day will pass.

So today, getting the chance to watch you for so long, was a red-letter day. Did you have a baby with you? I thought I saw you scoop one up at some stage, but then Nell came running up to the trees and I had to turn around briefly. You looked well, though. I should like to take your photograph like that. So happy and carefree, and waiting for me.

Yours,

M

192. LETTER FROM FLORENCE OLIVER TO LIZZIE CORN

Dear Lizzie,

You and I may be two useless old women, but we still have the power in us to make good things happen.

You should have seen the relief on Robyn's face when I handed over her file of dirty little stories. She'd only written about all of us, Lizzie. Even Brenda. "Did you read this?" she asked, and I shook my head, although of course I had. The one about Susan Reed at the circus made me laugh out loud, although I wouldn't like you to have seen what she said about Susan and the elephants.

It was the way she clutched the file to her as if it was another layer of protection she needed that made me lie.

"Want to see my secret?" I asked her then. I think I wanted her to know she wasn't alone in her shame. I took out one of my photographs from the envelope and handed it to her.

"Did he make you do this?" she said. She was touching the edge with her fingertips as if she didn't want to hold it at all, and I couldn't blame her. Luckily it wasn't the one where I was showing my whole back. Just peering a bit over my bad shoulder.

"No." It would have been easier to say yes, but I thought she deserved the truth. "I liked it."

She blinked twice. "I liked writing the stories too," she said, before straightening up. It was just how George did it. "You won't tell Mum, will you?"

"Not if you don't tell her about me." We should have shaken hands or something but we just nodded at each other, woman to woman.

"Is this what you wrote to Granddad about?" she said. "He never opened your letter, you know. He just looked at the file and told me to get rid of it, so I gave it to Steve."

"And the letter?" George and I had never mentioned it but it always felt as if it was there, hanging between us.

"I had a quick look and then I threw it away," she said, and I saw her cheeks go pink as she tried not to look at me. "Do you want me to get rid of them for you too?" She gestured toward the envelope but I shook my head.

"Not today," I said. So George had never seen my letter. I felt glad.

I didn't say anything about the letters to the mystery Mo I've got at the bottom of my wardrobe. I'll take them to the recycling units they have at the library and let Mo rest in peace.

She hugged me then, so tight she took my breath away. "You should get a tattoo," she said. "It would suit you."

How she makes me laugh. I nearly told her about you and Southend then, but I thought I'd gone far enough for one day.

"Just don't be ashamed," I said. "Whatever you do, never let anyone make you feel ashamed of it."

Now, Lizzie, let's think about you. You need a break. Let's say blow the lot of them and take ourselves off to Bournemouth as we'd planned. We'll stay in a hotel. A posh one where they turn back the sheets and give us little smelly soaps wrapped in tissue paper. We'll smile at all the grumpy teenagers like Robyn who other old ladies cross the street to avoid, and we'll eat mint choc ice creams with chocolate sprinkles, and take as long as we want getting around the mini golf. If anyone says anything nasty to us, we'll just snarl at them.

And every evening we'll go out dancing. Even if it's just to watch. Although I think we might take a few turns together, you and me.

Yours aye,

Flo

193. EMAIL FROM NELL BAKER TO ANGIE GRIFFITHS

Hey Angie,

Well, that's another mystery solved. Robyn's just shown me the file I saw in Martin's room. It's full of silly stories about the Pilgrims, even one about Dad dressing up in army uniform and spanking the ladies.

"Did you think it was funny?" I asked her, but she just shook her head. She said Martin made her do it.

We went out into the yard, built a bonfire and burned them all. Along with the original of that letter I scanned in for you.

"How did you get the file back?" I asked Robyn. I was thinking about those accusations of stealing.

"Someone gave it to me," she said, as if that was enough. And we both stoked the bonfire with big sticks, each getting rid of our demons. She's still out there, but I've come in to get things ready for you.

We shall see you later on tonight. We have lots to catch up on. Mark may pop around. Just warning you. He's taking up cooking. Nice to have a man around the kitchen again.

Nell

194. **ANSWER PHONE MESSAGE FROM**
ANGELA GRIFFITHS TO CLAUDE BICHOURIE

Claude, it's Angela. I'm sorry I didn't reply to your last letter but I was on the airplane when I suddenly realized I don't love you enough. I wanted to fly straight back to Paris and tell you because I don't want a financial arrangement, or a business arrangement, or any kind of arrangement between us anymore. I tried to get off the plane but they threatened to arrest me, and so here I am in England, at the airport, about to get into a taxi. I just want to be honest and straight with everyone. I want to take that risk now.

I'm on my way to see my father at last. For our child's sake.

195. **ANSWER PHONE MESSAGE FROM**
ANGIE GRIFFITHS TO NELL BAKER

Nell, it's me. I'm at the airport. Where is everyone? I'm going to see my father now. Wish me luck. And Nell, I love you. I'm sorry.

196. **LETTER FROM FLORENCE OLIVER TO LIZZIE CORN**

Dear Lizzie,

What a difference a week makes.

There I was with George yesterday when who should walk in but the French daughter. She'd come straight from the airport apparently with her suitcases and everything. I got up right away to leave them alone, of course, and I'd been in my room about an hour when there was a knock at the door. It was only her. She's the spit of Robyn, albeit with better clothes. The French know how to do seams. I read about it once.

"My father says you've been very kind to him," she said. And I don't know why, I'm still surprised at myself, but I found myself blubbering about how it was my fault he ended up in the hospital. I told her all about the photographs, and how I liked having them done, but then Martin ended up being so different from how he seemed, and how I showed them to Robyn too, just so she knew she wasn't alone, and how there was this box of letters to someone called Mo in his room too.

She sat down on my bed, and put her head in her hands. I thought, Flo, you are a silly old moo, you've only gone and upset someone else, but when she looked up she was laughing. Trying to hide it, but I could still see she was smiling.

"It was a photograph of one of my mother's friends that Martin showed him," she said.

"Your mother and her friend nude?"

And then she did laugh. She put her hand up to her mouth when she did and I was trying to think who else there was who did that gesture. "No," she said. "Just my mother's friend. My father seemed to think it would upset us if we knew that he had liked her once."

"And that was enough to put him in the hospital?"

"Are you ever too old to cry over love, Florence?" she asked then. I thought it was a strange comment, but as George would say, she's almost French now.

"Martin stole it," I said. "I stole things from your dad's room once too."

She looked a bit puzzled, and then nodded. "Yes," she said. "Martin took a lot of precious things once, but he can't get at them anymore." She's got this slight accent when she speaks, so it makes sense that she wears matching shoes and bags, you know, like the colonel's wife used to. She was foreign too, wasn't she? I kept pulling my skirt down. At least I was wearing the floral and false pearls so I could hold my own.

And then she asked me if I wanted her to get rid of the letters to the mystery Mo for me so I told her I'd already recycled them at the library. That's when I noticed the way she kept folding her hands over her stomach.

"George is going to have another grandchild," I said, and she blushed. Suddenly she didn't seem so French and haughty, but even more like Robyn. I wanted to give her a big hug and tell her it was going to be all right.

"He is," she said. "I've just told him, so he's busy trying to adjust right now. Although, it wasn't as hard as I thought it might be."

"It never is," I said. "Not when you finally get down to it."

It was later when I went up to Martin's empty bedroom, just to say good-bye, that I had a thought. I almost ran down to Brenda's room, nearly knocking Annabel over on my way. "Sexy lady," she called after me. "Beautiful saucy virgin." I was so excited I felt like hugging her too, but I was in too much of a rush.

"Brenda," I said, "when is the next resident moving in?"

She barely looked up from the desk. "Not for another month," she said.

So, Lizzie, what do you think? You could stay in Martin's room here for a month. It'll be better than Bournemouth. We will have peace when we want, and I'm sure we can persuade Steve to take us dancing. Maybe George could come too and just watch.

It'll be a fresh start. And we'll do ourselves some planning to see whether we can't sort out some way of getting Cora out of the house and you back with Laurie where you belong. We could even have ourselves a committee. George is awfully good at organizing, you'll see.

Yours aye,
Flo

Happily Ever After

Something Old

Six months later, George and Mrs. Oliver sat in silence on the lawn bench, ignoring the two small boys who peered over the wall. The couple were watching a bird peck at an empty coconut shell. The bird soon gave up, although the shell kept swinging for a long time afterward.

"Infinity," George said, and laughed.

"What are you going on about now, George?" Mrs. Oliver said, shifting closer to him. It was still too cold really to be sitting outside, but it was the first day of the year that the sun had some warmth in it. She put her face up, letting her body remember that life did come back. Green shoots that must be daffodil leaves were pushing up on the bank in front of them. It would be some time before the flowers came, but they would. Maybe even the cornflowers Martin planted last year. One day soon the yard would be full of color. How could she still be surprised by this every year?

"We were sitting here once when Martin asked me what I thought about infinity," George said.

"What did you tell him?"

"I didn't. Wish I had now. I'd tell him that I didn't believe in infinity. That's why it's important to make the most of the time you have now."

She was about to say something about all the things you could wish you'd said, but changed her mind. "Poor Martin," she said, and George nodded.

"Do you ever, you know, talking about wishes and stuff, feel guilty about what we're doing for Maureen's sake?" Florence's voice sounded strained, even to herself, and she didn't look at him. "I just need to ask you before the ceremony, particularly if we're thinking about Martin. You understand that, don't you?"

He stared up at the sky for a moment, before taking her hand. They relapsed into silence, and, from many years of practice with Graham, she tried to let that be enough.

Something New

Her baby was beautiful. Angela couldn't stop staring, touching, kissing. She counted his fingers, and his toes, his eyes, his ears, his knees. God, she wanted to eat him. To pop into her mouth the fist he kept waving in the air. It was hard to leave him alone.

A miracle.

And so much hair. A tuft of dark hair that she teased into a Mohawk and then into a unicorn's horn and then brushed down across his forehead. She lifted up his shirt, and blew a raspberry on his tummy.

Skin as soft as silk. And his smell. She traced a finger around the fontanel on the crown of his head, feeling how close she was to pressing right down to his inside. This gap would close up soon, Nell had told her. His skull would grow across and seal it, but now, for this minute, he was all hers. He'd no defenses. Maybe when he was older, she'd tell him about his real father, and his grandmother and grandfather, and how a sweetheart shot sometimes yielded unexpected results, but not until he was much older. And maybe not even then.

"You're Mummy's darling," she said. She blew another raspberry against his skin, just so she could hear him laugh. She wished Maureen had been able to hear it.

"Herr-hum."

Angela looked up. Nell and Robyn were standing at the doorway, smiling at her.

"Nearly ready?" Nell asked.

Angela took in Nell's silk dress. She knew instantly that Nell had chosen it with Mark in mind by the way it showed off her figure. God, Nell had changed. She was even walking with a wiggle nowadays. And Robyn had stopped looking like something out of a horror movie. The white pantsuit they'd chosen together was several hundred steps up from the dungarees Robyn normally insisted on. Angela looked at her watch.

"I haven't started to dress," she wailed. "I've been too busy."

"Auntie Angie," Robyn complained. "You've been up here for nearly an hour. Claude's already rung twice. He's at the church and he's worried you won't turn up."

"But the baby," Angela said, but Robyn had already scooped him up.

"I'm taking my cousin. Mum said you were always hopeless when there were men around," she said.

"She's right, Angie," Nell said. "We'll wait for you downstairs."

Angela gave up. It used to be bad enough standing her ground when it was just Nell, but she couldn't compete against two of them. She watched her son carried out of the room, and then turned to the mirror.

Besides, she had to admit she got a bit of a shock when she saw Nell standing there looking so good. She had some serious work to do before she was ready to go to the church.

Something Borrowed

James, Mark, and Steve were squashed up in the same pew.

They kept taking nervous glances at each other, saying nothing, not even when, in her role as usher, Lizzie Corn shuffled over to bring Angie's Frenchman to join them. They moved along the bench to give him room.

"The flowers, they are beautiful," Claude said loudly after nodding at them all, and they nodded back a touch too enthusiastically, although, in fact, it was only James who had noticed the flowers before.

"My daughter Robyn did them," he whispered back.

"And Nell," Mark added quickly.

The bouquets of red roses, heather, and huge tartan ribbons decorated the end of each pew, and a huge red-and-white arrangement stood at the altar. James would have included more green, he thought, to set off the wood, but he knew Nell and Robyn wouldn't have thought about that. He promised himself he wouldn't mention this to Robyn, but would just tell her what Claude had said and how proud it made him of her. He ignored Mark.

"George here yet?" Steve asked, and Mark shook his head.

"Not like him to be late," James said. "Did you all get your list of instructions?"

They nodded their heads.

"Wedding protocol, in bullet points," Mark said. "Both he and Florence have been driving Nell mad."

Suddenly, from the back of the church there was a scuffle and everyone turned around. When the music started, there were a few questioning looks at first and then people started to smile.

It was tango music. Loud, hot, and rhythmic. Suddenly in that cold English church those gathered started to dream of the sun, and of walking barefooted in the grass, and most of all, of the *passiono*.

Something Blue

Perhaps if George hadn't been late and hadn't had to run up the aisle to get there before them, Mrs. Oliver wouldn't have got the giggles. His red shirt was the final straw.

And if she hadn't laughed, she wouldn't have set Robyn off, or Nell, or Angie. And that wouldn't have made little baby George cry. They were like dominoes, or bowling pins. One ball upset them all.

From his position at the front of the church, still panting from his run, George tried to forget what he had just been praying for. Coming toward him were his girls. And they were walking willingly toward him, with everyone's blessing. Or nearly everyone's. He winked at Mrs. Oliver, and then turned quickly toward the altar and winked at that too, hoping his message would be carried up to Maureen. Just give me one sign, he prayed. Tell me he's not still bothering you. That we're all at peace now and this can be for real.

The priest came forward and held his arms up for silence. "Who givest this woman?" he asked.

Just any old sign, George asked. A beam of light, or a statue bleeding, that will do.

Nell and Angie took a step forward at exactly the same time, but when Angie automatically moved back to let her sister take over, Nell took her arm. "Not this time," she hissed, and she pushed Angie to the other side of Mrs. Oliver. "We do," she said. "Both of us, together." His daughters.

Maybe the roof could fall in, George thought, or the glass window could shatter. Or if you weren't feeling quite up to that, love, you could just turn the flowers blue. I didn't know about Martin. You should have felt able to tell me.

He gestured for Steve to come forward too as his best man, but somehow it seemed even better when the whole row of men mistook his signal, stood up and gathered around him. Angie's Frenchman, Claude, even kissed him, once on either cheek. George should have minded because this wasn't how things were done properly but he had other things on his mind. It was like a bloody party up there. A whole bloody committee, and then some.

I forgot people were more important, George prayed. So fell us all if you can't forgive me, but do it gently. Although, please, if you have any mercy, don't do it all. We don't want to go just yet. We've too much we want to do first.

He turned to Mrs. Oliver. How could he have been so stupid to risk her slipping away too? "Florence," he told her. "Let's take each other for better or worse."

Mrs. Oliver let out a belly laugh. "For worse, if you ask me," she said. "We're a pair of old fools, George. Look at you in that shirt."

The priest coughed, trying to bring their attention back to him. "We are gathered together here today," he started.

But he'd lost his audience. He hadn't done what George was always banging on about and stamped his authority on the meeting from the beginning. Standing up there, at the front of the church, handing the baby from one to another, jostling each other for space, congratulating and commiserating, the members of George's Committee, and then some, were like some music hall party who were in danger of bursting into song at any moment.

I meant no real harm, George prayed. I was just trying to survive. The best I knew how. I should have fought him off for you. Really tried to find out what was going on. Give us your blessing now.

But then, just as the priest was about to give up and shout at them all to come to order, peace was restored. It happened so suddenly, it was as if an unseen voice had told them all what to do. The rest of the party slipped back into their seats, and even the baby settled down. George and Florence came to stand before him, seriously and quietly.

"Did you bring a handkerchief? I don't do neat crying," Angela whispered in Nell's ear from the front pew, but Nell was busy wiping away her own tears on her coat sleeve. Angela took her sister's hand and squeezed it. She looked across at Claude. She'd tell him later she definitely wasn't coming back to Paris with him. Robyn was kissing the top of baby George's head as she promised she'd turn him into the perfect man, and she tried not to think about Martin. James was planning which houses he could introduce Robyn too that would get her interested in architecture again, and stop her needing to care about people so much. It wasn't healthy. Lizzie Corn was thinking how handsome Steve was and how a tall man made you feel safe. Troy was so small, surely Laurie would see sense while she was away. Claude was planning how he'd like his son to get married in an English church too one day, he and Angie standing proud at the front.

She'd see sense about this silly independence business. Next to him, Mark was working out how he was going to be able to drag Nell away after the service. God, she was looking hot.

The vicar looked at the wedding couple. When he first heard their ages, he'd thought this all might be a quaint story he could use in a sermon, but this had turned out to be the strangest wedding he'd ever had to officiate at, what with the groom in his red shirt and the bride winking at everyone, that tango music and all those ghastly relatives. Plus they'd requested the whole service. The bride had insisted even on the begetting bit; they could still have some fun trying, apparently. Although he doubted, surely not, what with their joint ages nearing two hundred. "A marriage," he began, "is a sacred thing. Not to be entered into lightly."

George and Florence nodded fiercely at him.

"Get on with it then," demanded Mrs. Oliver. "We haven't got all that long left and we want to enjoy ourselves in what little time we have. Don't we, George?" She nudged her husband-to-be painfully in the ribs.

He tried not to wince, and that's when he got it. His sign. It didn't come in the form of broken windows, or shafts of light, or even blue flowers. And that's how he knew it came from Maureen. Because big gestures had never been her style. No, the sign she had sent could all too easily have been overlooked. It was Florence's elbow in his side, and all those faces in the front rows, and all the pilgrims three too, laughing along with them both. And how no one was looking over their shoulder anymore. George felt a sense of peace, one he hadn't felt for a long time.

"We do," he told the shocked vicar, who had never in his life been interrupted quite so much. "For bloody infinity, however long that may last."

Acknowledgments

Grateful thanks are due to the many people who kept me going in different ways, both large and small, while I was writing this book including, Mary Atkinson, Christopher Barker, Nicholas Bate, Billie Bolton, Café Divine, the Clink Steet group, Alice Elliot Dark, Sue Davis, Carlos Ferguson, Neil Gaiman, Alison Grant, Deborah Heath, Rupert Heath, Will Hermes, Celia Hunt, James Friel, Alex Johnson, Anne Kelly, Shaun Levin, Michelle Lovric, Mo McAuley, Cheryl Moskowitz, Scott Pack, Reginald Peplow, Lynne Rees, Hugh Salway, Rachael Salway, Laura Sampson, Rebecca Shapiro, Catherine Smith, Christine Terris, Susan Wicks, and everyone at the Virginia Center for Creative Arts.

PHOTO: © MICHAEL WILDSMITH

SARAH SALWAY is the author of two novels, *The ABCs of Love* and *Tell Me Everything* (Ballantine Books), and a collection of short stories, *Leading the Dance* (Bluechrome). She lives in London, and is currently the Royal Literary Fund Fellow at the London School of Economics and Political Science. Her website is www.sarahsalway.net.